James D. Law

Dreams o' Hame and other Scotch Poems

James D. Law

Dreams o' Hame and other Scotch Poems

ISBN/EAN: 9783744707909

Printed in Europe, USA, Canada, Australia, Japan

Cover: Foto ©Andreas Hilbeck / pixelio.de

More available books at **www.hansebooks.com**

Dreams o' Hame

AND OTHER

Scotch Poems

(With a few Experiments in English Verse)

BY

JAMES D. LAW

Camden, N.J., U.S. America

Gi'e me ae spark o' nature's fire!
That's a' the learnin' I desire;
Then tho' I drudge thro' dub and mire
    At pleugh or cart,
My muse, tho' hamely in attire,
    May touch the heart.—*Burns.*

ALEXANDER GARDNER
Publisher to Her Majesty the Queen

PAISLEY; AND PATERNOSTER SQUARE, LONDON

1893

To

Scots Abroad

THIS BOOK

I DEDICATE.

JAMES LAW.

Proem.

WHEN I consider how the world is bor'd by scribbling fellows who are much my betters, and how it
dotes upon the countless horde of titled magnates in
the field of letters, I wish to goodness I had been a
lord; for all my chances of success it fetters to look
for money (not to mention fame) without a handle
to my sorry name.*

I'm not a writer like a skilled attorney or penny-
liner for the daily press; I've no acquaintance with
the art of Gurney or Isaac Pitman, and I must confess I like to loiter on a pleasant journey, and let my
pencil or my pen digress: there's entertainment in a
shady by-way that's never met with on the dusty
highway. I'm not a pedant, so the spots and specks
you are apt to meet with in a modern print, within
my volume they shall never vex you; the learn'd
allusion and the classic hint—with these let scholars

*in their works perplex you, I say there's naught but ostentation in't, although an author that can use such phrases stands high, I notice, in his readers' praises.**

*Then, criticasters, that are overstocked with all the polish that the Age disperses, I give you warning, get your muskets cocked ; a candid poet now so very scarce is, it's not unlikely that you may be shocked before you finish with my rustic verses ; so, while your nerves are in a manner steady, take my advice and get your weapons ready. And, gentle public, that delights to feast on namby-pamby and insipid twaddle, the Pegasus I for the nonce have leased is unaccustomed to the rein or saddle, the noble steed is such a healthy beast, the very moment that I get astraddle my skill's devoted, not to frills and scallops, but how to sit him as he soars and gallops. A simple man, I sing for simple folk, in simple language and in simple strain ; my rhyming talent is my total stock, and thus equipped I venture on the main.—O guard me, Muses, from the storm and rock, until the harbour I shall make again, for when I'm sailing on a doubtful sea a hidden snag might play the deuce with me.**

So, as I hinted, for my volume's sake I wish I were but titled, rich, or dead—for then my venture would be no mistake, and all my writings would be widely read; but at the present I am wide-awake, I've wife and children to be clothed and fed: a situation that's perhaps pathetic, but unromantic as it's unpoetic.

And yet it has been said, and said with truth, an audience can be found for any theme: a bard who scribbles in a style uncouth, to certain people will perfection seem: be but eccentric, and your work, forsooth, tho' skim-milk only, may be class'd as cream; it takes all classes to make up a nation, and so in tastes there must be variation. Some folks think delf-ware is the finest pottery, and mediocrity the mass commends; the poorest writers can command a coterie, so I may also have my troop of friends; I'll take my chances in the Printers' Lottery, for, as some author of repute contends, No man's unlucky till his luck he tries, and who can tell but I may draw a prize!

.•. There's always more than on the surface shines! Remember, reader, if you would abuse them, some collocations of prosaic lines are all-essential, or I would not use them. For those

not posted on my true designs, I hope this note may at the least amuse them, knowing that those who penetrate the mask can justly value my stupendous task.   O, feat exacting, that should so restrict the frolic fancy of my roving pen, and make me all-unwillingly inflict such mysticisms on my fellow-men ; but tarry, critic, till the lock is picked (and I'm contented to lie low till then), because, tho' scored now for my ambiguity, I'll yet be worshipped for my ingenuity.   I know it's vulgar to descend to slang, for slang has meaning to the vulgar only, yet thereby, reader, doth a cipher hang to vex the patience of some future Donnelly : I shall not bore you with a long harangue, but Shakespeare stands among the bards so lonely, to keep him company (such as I am !) I've thro' my Poems run a Cryptogram !   This frank expression may explain, I hope, some puzzling phrases in my rhythmic chimes, and help my students when for gold they grope amongst the statements that I make at times.   It is not every Poet that can cope with rhymes below the surface of his rhymes : between the lines a tale is often spun, but underneath the lines—ah, there's the fun !

CONTENTS.

xiv. *Contents.*

Contents.

DREAMS O' HAME.

A DREAM O' HAME.

(Part I.—Geographical.)

" We shall conduct you to a hill . . ., laborious indeed at the
first ascent, but else so smooth, so green, so full of goodly prospects,
and melodious sounds on every side, that the harp of Orpheus was not
more charming."

Noo *Phœbus'* spear has turned adrift
The darklin' cloods that thrang'd the lift ;
The hinmost Cock has wound his Horn
An' flegg'd awa' the Mists o' Morn ;
The fragrant Winds aroond me blawn
Hae drench'd wi' Dew the fiery Dawn,
And diamond draps in clusters rowe
Frae ilka Blade and Bush and Bough.

Aboon wi' Girss and Heather hap
Auld *Noth* uprears his Sphinx-like *Tap ;*—
The Watch-Dog o' the Rock-bound North,
And grandest Hill ayont the Forth !

Frae *Rhynie* couch'd beside its paws
I start to clim' the tow'rin' wa's :
Aince mair I pass the massive rock
That bears the print o' *Giant Jock ;*
Walk roun' the *Crag o' Clochmaloo,*
And perchin' pick my pathway thro'
The breastworks built o' birsl't stanes
That dootless hap some Royal Banes,
Until I reach the Cup or Cap
That croons the summit o' the *Tap,*
And keps the dews at morn and e'en
That keep the Cone for ever green !

Lo, what a cycloramic view
Is spread for miles before me noo !

A Dream o' Hame.

What wealth of Sea and Hill and Dale,

Of Highland Moor and Lowland Vale ;

Of Streams that twine like siller threids

Thro' Mossy Haughs and Grassy Meads ;

Of Roads that in their twists and turns

Look like the beds of dried up Burns ;

What gowden glints of Whinny Howes,

Of Wavin' Corn and Broomy Knowes ;

What blinks o' Castles and o' Kirks

Embower'd in Beeches and in Birks ;

Of Touns that flash upon the sicht

Like stars upon a cloudless nicht ;

Of Clachans, Steadin's, Crafts, and Cots,

Ilk wi' their little Kail-yard Plots ;—

O, I could stand, and nae be loth,

For days upon the *Tap o' Noth*,

And gaze across its saucer-rim

Till sense would reel and sicht grow dim ;

And ye could scour auld Scotland o'er,

Yea, Britain braid itsel' explore,

And trudge for mony a month, I ween,
To match me sic a glorious scene !

Ben Rinnes lonely in the West
Uprears his kingly guardian crest ;
And to the East is stretch'd afar
A Glen without a peer or par,—
Strathbogie wi' its fertile haughs,
Its aucht-and-forty famous daughs,
Immortalized in Scottish lore,
The grand old Gordon Land of yore !

A bit beyond I clearly see
Culsalmond, Foudland, Bennachie ;
The *Garioch* and the *Buchan* lands,
The *Mormond Hill* that mateless stands,
And like a ghaist may be descried
The *White Horse* built upon its side !

Noo glow'rin o'er the *Kirkney Glen*
Whaur sleep brave Lulach's thousand men,

I pierce the reek frae coontless fires

And rest on *Huntly's* Towers and Spires,

By which the *Bogie's* waters glide

Half-feart in *Deveron's* drumlier tide !

Far Eastwards on the *Banffshire Coast*

The Land within the Sea is lost,

And Northwards as my een I turn

I see the *Knock* and *Hill o' Durn*,

The *Cullen* and the *Cairnie Binns*

Wi' smilin' fields alang their shins,

And then anither blink o' blue

When *Moray's Firth* bursts into view !

Athwart the waters o' the Bay,

Whaur Fishin'-Smacks their sails display,

I note the shadowy *Hills o' Ross*,

That to the cloods their tap-knots toss,

And glimmerin' far ayont them a'

The *Paps o' Caithness* fade awa' !

I change my place again and gaze

At *Essie's Burn* and *Essie's Braes ;*

Knock Caillich wi' the huddrey heid,

The theme o' mony a mystic screed

When Witches on their broom-sticks rode

And Warlocks walked the Earth abroad !

Far Sooth the lordly *Grampians* rise

Like hay-stacks set against the skies ;

And mony a noble peak I see

Aroond the Straths o' *Upper Dee.*

O, what a stretch o' Wood and Glen

Frae *Lochnagar* to *Clochnaben,*

And what a world o' Dale and Doun

Frae *Mount o' Keen* to *Morven's* croon !

Noo fondly turn my eyes to Hame

And a' my blood is changed to flame.:

O'er a' the Hills I see the *Buck*

His tap as snod's a weel trimmed ruck ;

Encompass'd roun' wi' Mosses black

The *Cabrach* snugglin' at his back;

And look hoo couthie in his airms

He hauds braw *Clova's* Woods and Fairms;

And then to mak' the scene complete

Lythe *Lumsden* cuddlin' at his feet,

Wi' lang *Coreen* outstretched beyon'

Betwixt the *Dev'ron* and the *Don !*

Entranced, I catch upon the breeze

The Bleat o' sheep, the Bum o' Bees;

The Whirrin' o' a Pairtrick's Wings;

The Gurglin' o' the Mountain Springs;

The steady Swish frae aff a Scythe;

A Shepherd Whistlin' bauld and blythe;

The Sough o' Winds that sway the Woods;

The Lilts o' Larks that cleave the Cloods;

A Studdie Ringin' doun the Howe;

Frae nibblin' Nowte an' antrin Low;

And like the sharp and rhythmic Note

Frae some gigantic Cricket's throat

The mesured Dirge of Death that's borne

Frae Reapers stalkin' thro' the Corn !

Aince mair I rove amang the scenes

That aft hae cheer'd me in my 'teens ;

I start aboon the *Burn o' Craig*

And thro' its wooded *Den* stravaig ;

I muse beside its *Castle* wa',

And watch its foamin' waters fa' ;

I pass the *Auld Kirk* ivied o'er

Whaur sleep the deid o' *Auchindoir ;*

Then by *Glenbogie's* woods I stray

Whaur Nature dons her best array ;

Whaur stands romantic *Corbie Tongue* ·

By Painters lov'd, by Poets sung ;

Whaur Birks hang oot their tassels free

To deck the cliffs beside *Win'see,*

And whaur the Freestane *Quarry Howe*

Wi' gowden bloom is fair alowe !

Syne *Bogie* skirts the Sculptur'd Stanes

Erected on the *Fairm o' Mains ;*
Jouks by the *Knowe* whaur records tell
The kirk-fowk rang the Parish Bell,
And whaur in ages lang awa'
The Druids held their Courts o' Law ;
Then saft and slow the burnie glides
By a' the various *Bogie-sides,*
In hailin' distance o' the wood
That hauds *Druminnor's* turrets prood ;
And whaur the saughs like siller gleam
It joins the *Essie's* ripplin' stream !

Thro' *Rhynie* still it winds alang
And sings its gentle, cheerfu' sang ;
By *Lochrie* snug and *Smiston* cauld ;
By *Noth's* twin touns, the *New* and *Auld ;*
The *Cults,* the *Kirkney* and the *Ness*
Contendin' for the first caress ;
Syne doon the *Strath* it tak's its course,
(Whaur snorts and roars the Iron Horse),

Wi' mony a lazy twirl and twine,

And aft a backward swirl and sweel,

Betwixt the *Turnpike* and the *Line*,

As if 'twas wae to say Fareweel ! *

---

* See Appendix A.

A DREAM O' HAME.

(*Part II.—Historical.*)

"A tale of the times of old !
The deeds of days of other years !"

MAJESTIC Tap ! in mony a tome
That tells the feats o' haughty Rome ;
In Celtic runes, if not in rhymes ;
In tales of Ossianic times ;
In sangs of Norse and Danish Scald
Thy sons' heroic deeds are tauld,
When Pictish kings held Royal Court
Within thy fire-cemented fort !
Well may thy breast be strewn with scars,
Spectator of a thousand wars ;
And proudly may you raise your head
Aboon the Bogie's crystal bed,

For all unconquered still you stand,
The glory of our northern land !

Across thy glen in thousands deep
Ye've seen the Roman soldiers sweep ;
Ye've seen them build their roads an' wa's
That still defy Time's ruthless claws ;
And ye ha'e seen thy native hordes,
Wi' twig-twined shields and pointless swords,
Swoop down on wings of wind and flame,
And drive the Imperial Eagles hame !

Again ye've seen and yet again
The Scandinavian and the Dane .
Rush through thy fair and fertile strath,
And leave destruction in their path.
O burns of blood ye've witness'd spilt
In broils betwixt the Pict and Celt ;
But in the end they cam' to gree,
And tamed the Rovers of the Sea !

Then in the gentler times of peace,

When clang and clash of arms would cease,

Ye've heard the blue-eyed maiden sing

By babblin' burn or bubblin' spring,

As in the dusk of eve or morn

She turned the quern and ground the corn.

And ye hae watch'd amang thy knowes

The Druid priests perform their vows ;

Hae seen the blood-red fires of Baal

Flash oot their licht across thy vale ;

And seen the sacred knife uprise

That reek'd wi' human sacrifice,

Amidst the shouts of Pagans pleased,

Who thus believed their gods appeased.

When closed his kingly eyes in death

Ye saw the army of Macbeth

Dejected cross the Rhynie " meers,"

Pursued by Malcolm's vengefu' spears.

Preceded by his brithers twa,

Ye saw the gallant Lulach fa',

And, in the licht frae Luna's horn,

Ye saw his princely body borne,

Amid a nation's grief and gloom,

To far Iona's royal tomb.

Then cam' the fechts betwixt the Kirks,

When Christian love was taught by dirks !

And then the wars by Edward brocht,

When Scots for Independence focht !

Ay, those " wha hae wi' Wallace bled,"

On Bogie's banks hae made their bed ;

And there, too, has the regal Bruce

At times thought fit to introduce

The gallant and devoted band

That shed new lustre on our land.

Sair day was that when up the howe

Ye saw Kildrummy Castle's lowe ;

When Scotland's Queen was held in chains

A captive in her ain domains ;

When on the brave Sir Nigel's head

The carrion Sass'nach curs were fed,

To please a craven English lord

Who failed to conquer by his sword ;

And sweet the day when frae your seat

Ye saw the Southrons in retreat,

And heard oor valiant King declare

That they should vex oor land nae mair !

And then ye've seen in later days

The Forbes and the Gordon frays,

And witness'd a' the plots and plans

Of these uncompromising clans.

How each, at times, in friendship's guise,

Would tak' their neighbours by surprise ;

Invite them to the festive board

And chant the praise of peace restored ;

And when wi' feastin' and wi' fun

The unsuspecting guests were won,

When feuds were drowned in friendly din,

Behold ! the host would stroke his chin,

And ilka man that claimed him chief,

Wi' glitterin' blade and parley brief,

Would wale his foe wi' skill expert,

And plunge the steel within his he'rt !

And aft ye've smiled upon the scenes

Of rustic mirth on village greens,

Like those of which—in stanzas lang—

Our Royal Minstrel * sweetly sang ;

Nay, were ye not Parnassus Mount,

Thy spring the true Castalian fount,

And " Christe's Kirk " lilt the sweet reward

That blessèd the youthful Sovereign Bard ?

When Donald, Lord of all the Isles,

Misled by fortune's fickle smiles,

---

* King James I. of Scotland.

Ambitious, daring, and alone,

Laid siege upon the Scottish throne,

Ye saw your loyal-hearted men

In thousands leave their native glen,

And help the rebels' necks to thraw

Upon the field o' red Harlaw.

On mony a blood-stained battle-plain

Thy stalwart sons have held their ain,

When, from the mountains of the North,

The Fiery Cross has called them forth :

Bear witness, ill-starred Flodden field,

Where Huntly was the last to yield ;

Bear witness, Tillieangus heath,

Wi' mony a hero stretch'd beneath ;

Glenlivet, where the base Argyll

Got first his taste o' Bogie's style ;

And mony a Covenantin' raid,

Whaur waved the dark-green tartan plaid,

And whaur the " Byd——and—— ! " slogan cry
Proclaimed the dauntless Gordons nigh !

In 'Fifteen, when the Earl o' Mar
Unfurl'd the flag of civil war,
Ye saw your best, amidst applause,
Espouse the Royal Stuart's cause ;
And in defeat ye saw wi' pain
Kildrummy's towers ablaze again,
And " Scotland's richtfu' king " depairt
An exile wi' a broken he'rt !

Still Huntly kept her love alive,
And in the grander 'Forty-five
Her rank and file with one accord
For Bonnie Charlie drew the sword.
But woe to Clan Macdonald dour
That lost the Prince Drumossie Moor ;
Soon in the heart of Bogie's glen
Was heard the tramp of George's men,

And grimly did they slake their steel

And show their Hanoverian zeal,

By bringin' wrack an' death on a'

That mourned the Highland laddie's fa'!

Thus closed the age of sturt an' strife,

And better times sprang into life :

Nae mair within Strathbogie's bounds

The pibroch blast of war resounds ;

Whaur ance the ruler was the sword

The plough is noo acknowledged lord ;

Noo cornfields wave whaur standards streamed :

Noo scythe-blades flash whaur spears aince gleamed ;

The fairm-horse tak's the war-horse' pairt ;

The chariot's yielded to the cairt ;

Whaur bullets whizzed, noo engines shriek ;

Whaur cannons smoked, noo hooses reek ;

In peacefu' tilts the people strive,

And at their simple labours thrive ;

Work blythely in the braid day-licht,

And sweetly, soundly sleep at nicht,

Unvex'd by ony o' the ills

That ever stalked amang the hills

Or flourished in the bygone days

Within the vale that Noth surveys!

So may it be till ne'er a drap

Of Bogie's ripplin' burn is seen!

So may it be until the Tap

Is level wi' the Rhynie Green!

And till the day of which I sing,

As on their course the ages rowe,

May ilka year mair pleasure bring

To a' that live within the howe,

Which, tho' it's far beyond the faem!

I'll aye be prood to ca' my hame!

PROLOGUE TO SCOTTISH CONCERT.

(*Philadelphia, Pa., U.S. America.*)

" A NIGHT of Scottish Song ! "
At mention of the phrase
What visions rise before our eyes
Of home and early days !

Once more we see the heath-clad hills
Tower grandly to the skies,
And, massed like cloods, the Autumn woods
Display their myriad dyes !
We see the burnie wind alang
Its journey to the sea,
And hear it sing its auld-time sang
Of mingled grief and glee !

Again the merle, wi' silver throat,

　　Rings gloamin' o'er the lawn,

And lav'rocks pipe their golden note

　　Exultant to the dawn !

Anew for us the daisies bloom,

　　And all their charms unfold,

Afresh we scent the whins and broom

　　That deck the dells with gold !

The bosky glens and shady dens,

　　Where nods the wild blue-bell,

The quarry knowes and fairy howes—

　　What tales of love they tell !

What blinks of sweet and sonsy maids,

　　Red cheeks and sparklin' een ;

Of sporran'd kilts and tartan plaids,

　　And gallants on the green !

Bless Scotia's glorious mother-tongue,

　　Revered at home, abroad ;

Its tales are told, its songs are sung,

    Where'er man's foot hath trod !

In tropic climes, 'mang Arctic snaws,

    It sheds its fragrance roun';

Yea, ilka breath o' wind that blaws

    Is balmy wi' its soun' !

What Caledonian can withstan'

    The glamourie o' its lays?

What Clansman, worthy of his clan,

    Who would not swell its praise ?

While running waters seaward roll,

    Its melodies divine

Shall fire the blood and stir the soul

    As in the *auld lang syne !*

THE MERRY QUAKERS!

(Philadelphia Scottish Games.)

HOOCH! siccan lilts frae pipers braw
  On Monday we'll be hearin',
E'er Phœbus o'er the City Ha'
  Will hae his colts careerin';
Then Caledonian clansmen a'
  Will jump their Highland gear in,
  And croose in croods be steerin'
For Pastime Park awa'!

O, leeze me on the Pibroch's croon,
  It breathes o' hill and heather!
The weary Scot, wi' care cast doun,
  Loups lichtsome as a feather

When some auld saul-inspirin' tune

    Comes birlin' frae the blether,

    And wha need try to tether

The Celt that hears the soun'?

Noo City Fathers, City Dames,

    And Young Folks a', I tent ye,

Speed to the Park and leave your Hames

    And heaviness ahint ye;

And I'll avooch ye'll vaunt its claims

    While memory's charm is lent ye,

    And bless the bard that sent ye

To see the Scottish Games!

To start, sic dandies there will be

    At hoochin' and at dancin',

The kilties knappin' on the knee,

    The belts an' buckles glancin';

The plaids an' ribbons furlin' free,
Rainbows o' claith the stance in—
O, gin ye there should chance in,
Be sure that sicht ye see !

Some haimmers fling, some putt the stanes,
Some try to toss the caber ;
There, jumpin' some wad brak' their banes
To triumph o'er a neighbor,
And records ding to smithereens
As cleanly as a sabre,.
Or aix frae far Lochaiber
Would strip a pine o' preens !

And siccan fun it is to view
The rinnin' and the racin' ;
Some fleet as fallow deer, I troo,
Oot o'er the hurdles chasin',

Some tied in bags up to the mou'

On to the landin' pressin',

And some, three-leggit, pacin'

In hopes a prize to pu' !

While here, like cushie-doos in line,

Quoits for the mote are wingin' ;

There Dons at *Ghillie Callum* fine

High han's an' heels are flingin' ;

Syne at the close the band they join,

In mighty chorus singin',

And thro' the field sen' ringin'

Auld Scotia's *Auld Langsyne* !

Noo, City Fathers, City Dames,

And Young Folks a', I tent ye,

Speed to the Park and leave your Hames

And heaviness ahint ye ;

And I'll avooch ye'll vaunt its claims

While memory's charm is lent ye,

And bless the bard that sent ye

To see the Scottish Games !

TO A MOSQUITO.

ILL-TRICKIT, wickit, bizzin' beastie,
Nae langer on my face ye'll feast ye!
Sin' noo my thoom-nail I've got neist ye,

   Yer banes will rattle;
And troth it's time I should arreist ye,

   And gar ye sattle.

I'm far frae sorry, snip, to fin' ye,
And tho' my blood may course within ye,
Wi' lattin'-aff I'll nae begin ye,—

   That wad be sport ill;
For while the cannibal is in ye,

   We would assort ill.

I dootna but ye'll ca' me knave,

An' owre my whunstane rancour rave ;

And fegs, I maybe misbehave,

   But, crater, bless ye,

I'll get my sairin' o' the lave,

   And never miss ye.

Ye ken it's a' your ain misdoin',

That sent me aifter you pursuin' ;

Had ye been less intent tatooin'

   Ye micht hae seen

The ruthless claws that wrocht yer ruin,

   And dodged atween.

But na ! ye had ta'en nae forecast,

An' frae yer feast ye wadna fast ;

Snug, safe frae ilka by-gaun blast

   Ye thocht yersel',

Till thud ! the foe cam' doon at last,

   An' broke your spell.

Nae mair I'll nip aneath yer nibbles,

Nae mair ye'll bore me wi' yer gibbles,

Nae mair ye'll draw my bluid in dribbles,

   Or gar't rin cauld !

Ae stammack less will stress my stibbles,

   Ye glutton bauld !

But 'Skeeter ! thou art nabb'd alane,

Frae lots o' cronies—provin' plain

Mosquitoes' schemes, like schemes o' men,

   Are deep laid aye !

Whaur a'e rogue happens to be ta'en,

   A score win by !

Still you're weel aff, compared wi' me ;

Your doom is—jist at aince to dee !

An' forward tho' I canna see,

   I sadly fear

That I may claw 'neath sic as thee,

   For mony a year !

EPISTLE TO JAMES W. R. COLLINS.

WHAT's the maitter noo, dear Jamie?
　Truly it's a sorry case!
Ne'er a letter noo comes ti' me,
　Let alane to see your face!

Are ye noo forbid to toddle
　Ony mair your frien's to see?
Laddie, what's come owre your noddle
　That you keep sae far frae me?

A' last week I thocht to see ye,
　Or at least to get a line,
Tellin' hoo the warl' went wi' ye,—
　Sour an' dour, or fair and fine.

But as weel expect a thoosan'
  Poun's frae aff a tree to pu',
As to get a minute's newsin',
  Wi' a busy chiel like you !

.   .   .   .   .   ,

Things are aye the same in Camden,
  Canty are we a' and crouse,
Happier here by far than cramm'd in
  Some sma' Philadelphia hoose !

Winter's back is fairly broken,
  Birds again begin to sing,
And their happy strains betoken,
  Promise of an early Spring !

Trees that like demented bodies,
  Naked, braved the wintry storms,
In the wealth o' Summer duddies,
  Soon will deck their varied forms !

3

But the subject noo to vary,

    Lest I tire ye o' my skeel—

What's the news aboot Mt. Airy ?—

    Wife an' bairns I trust are weel ?

.   .   .   .   .

I—but noo my jaded Musie

    Hints it's time my pen to dicht ;

I'll alloo I'm gettin' droosy,

    So I guess I'll say Gude-Nicht !

March, 1892.

UP AN' WAUR THEM A', WILLIE!

*(Inscribed to General William T. Sherman, and read by
Mr. Andrew Carnegie at the New York Burns
Celebration, 1890.)*

Up an' waur them a', Willie!
　Up an' waur them a',
In mony a splore ye've done't afore
　Withoot a bit to blaw, Willie!
Ye crack'd the croons o' thrawart loons,
　And laid them doon the law, Willie,
By deed an' word—by pen an' sword,
　Till nane daur'd say ye ' Na,' Willie!

Up an' waur them a', Willie!
　Up an' waur them a',
In fields o' war a brichter star
　Than yours we never saw, Willie!

And noo in peace ye shine, the same
   As in the years awa', Willie,
Wi' spotless fame and deathless name,
   The brawest o' the braw, Willie !

Up an' waur them a', Willie !
   Up an' waur them a',
The valiant warrior Scots of old,
   Your glorious feats reca', Willie !
Ye took command that better days
   For rich and poor micht daw', Willie,
And South and North they sing your worth,
   In Cottage and in Ha', Willie !

Up an' waur them a', Willie !
   Up an' waur them a',
Wi' leave to follow at your heel,
   Withoot a thocht ava', Willie,

We'd nae be fley'd to face the Deil,

And gie his neck a thraw, Willie,—*

O, he that winna wish ye weel,

Misfortune be his fa', Willie !

Up an' waur them a', Willie !

Up an' waur them a',

Thrice worthy o' Columbia's praise,

And Caledon's hurrah, Willie !

May ye hae wealth o' happy days,

Hoots !—Years a score or twa, Willie,

And gin the Fates should send ye faes

Up an' waur them a', Willie !

---

* In a note acknowledging copy of Poem, the gallant old veteran wrote "I hope to outflank the Deil for some years yet."

OOR BAIRNIE.

O, WE hae got a bairnie,
　Noo twice a towmond auld,
And tho' I wrote a beukfu',
　His worth could nae be tauld ;
He's worth the hale wide warl',
Oor curly-heided bairnie—
　. There ne'er was sic a carle.

And we hae had oor bairnie
　Richt nearly frae us ta'en,
And couldna tell the joy we felt
　When he cam' roun' again ;
When he cam' roun' aince mair,
Oor bonnie lauchin' bairnie
　That Death saw fit to spare !

Lang life to you, dear bairnie,
  And ilka good that gangs
To those that lichten labour,
  And saften poortith's stangs !
May Fate for you provide,
In proper time sic bairnie
  To brichten your fireside !

WHAUR SUMMER DAYS ARE LANG.

(Kincluny, Durris, by the Dee.)

THEIR day's wark past they noo convene
To test upon the village green,
Or some bit field upon the fairm
Their speed o' fit and strength o' airm !

Within the lythe o' yon dykeside,
Wi' vetchy, girss an' gowans pied,
His collie couched his legs between
The fairmer views the sportive scene.
Nae Show within a Playhouse wa's
Whaur Puppets strut to win applause,
But Nature's bairns, weel-knit, weel-faur'd,
Disportin' on the velvet sward !

To beat the record unco fain

Here's Sandy strugglin' wi' the Stane :

Upon ae fit he mintin' stan's,

The wish'd-for point sedately scans,

Syne bangin' up against the butt

Wi' a' his pith put in the putt,

Forth like a flash the Stane lats fung

That owre the foremost dings the dung !

There, Jamie jumpin' at the bar,

And fley'd he canna rise sae far,

Strips aff his claes to sark an' breeks,

A stick in ilka nivelock cleeks,

An rushin' forrit, fierce as win',

Determination in his chin,

Tak's in the heicht wi' practis'd e'e,

Syne wi' a jerk that few can gie

Gangs owre the ploo-rein like a bird

An' wi' a yark fa's in the yird !

Heck yonder at the Haimmer flings,

Thrice roun' his head the wheel-bush swings,

Syne lats it lowss wi' a' his micht

And gars it some twa inches licht

Oot owre the farrest " clean-throw " mark

That has been notit by the Clark ;

A hint as Heck nae blate proclaims

To try his luck at neist years Games,

For he micht prove the chiel to win

The Championship frae Davidson !

O, happy are they ane an' a' !

Some pitch the wechts, some bat the ba' ;

Some rax their legs—hop-step-and-leap ;

Some rin till in a sweat they dreep ;

Some thro' the core on stilparts stump ;

Some shoeless, hoseless, close-fit jump ;

Some brak' the posts and pailin' bars

In tossin' cabers to the stars ;

Bob, vaunty, vaultin', pole in han',

Will tak' nae tips frae ony man ;

Some tak' a canny game at Quoits,

(The king o' sports for skill's exploits !)

Frae clay to clay to mak' a score

For 'oors they trachle back an' fore,

Debatin' "points" an' "ringers" won,

Till darkness gars them quit the fun.

For noo Mirk on the scene has crap

The sun's lang sunk o'er Morven's Tap ;

The stars are startin' frae the cloods,

The owls are hootin' thro' the woods ;

Rats frae the rucks begin to peer,

And for the dam their courses steer ;

Doun in the sandy, saughy heugh

Dee seems to rin wi' safter sough ;

Frae mossy bogs the puddicks croak,

Syne tykes to stint o' barkin' yoke ;

The bauky bird flees roun' their heids

As frae the field the auld man leads

And to the kitchy or the barn,

His booit blinkin' like a starn,

Conveys them whaur the lasses free

Are met to help gar evening flee !

There to the fiddler's rantin' strain,

They dance and rest and dance again ;

Unvex'd by warldly cark or care,—

Noo here a Speech, noo there a Sang,—

The whyle they are forgaither'd there

As happy as the days are lang !

PSALM I.

Tune—French.

BLESS'D is the man that tak's nae stock
　In what the godless say;
Wha wadna trock wi' sinfu' folk,
　Nor seek to walk their way!

Wha sitsna in the big bow-chair
　The scornfu' like to fill,
But mak's his care aye mair and mair
　To work the Maister's will!

Wha never tynes it frae his sicht
　At hame or far awa',
But in daylicht and in midnicht
　Keeps thinkin' on God's law!

That man shall flourish like the tree
    That grows beside a burn,
Whaur fruit we see aye hingin' free
    As summer days return !

A tree whose leaves shall ne'er be lost
    Tho' ithers' boughs be clean,
But braw may boast thro' sun and frost
    A glossy robe o' green !

That man may gang to sell or buy
    And still good luck command,
Yea, may rely whate'er he try
    Shall prosper in his hand !

But nae the men that Conscience droon
    And steep themsel's in sin,
They'll stoyter roun' till they gang doon
    Like stooks afore the win' !

Nor will the wicked be alloo'd

    In Paradise to dwell,

For God hath voo'd nane but THE GOOD

    Shall sit beside Himsel'!

A NICHT WI' BURNS.

To the Tune of "Cauld Kail Het Owre Again."

O, WHA can put in words the pain a book-worm has to
  bear

When some rare gem, lang socht in vain, is met and
  miss'd aince mair !

And whatna tongue can tell the joy that in a capture
  lies ?—

It's pleasure pure, withoot alloy, to him wha pu's the
  prize.

On sic a catch the tither nicht, in HIGHLAND'S book-
  rooms braw,

By some expert's rare oversicht it was my luck to fa' :

'Auld Caledon's *Antiquities*; by Captain Francis Grose'—

Sae plentiful in things to please, sae scant in fau'ts to
  gloze !

As in the garret by mysel' I daur'd its worth to pree,

It tookna lang to cast the spell of aulden times on me.

I soon was wafted to the days when Pencil, Pen and
 Sword

Commingled in a glorious blaze around Glenriddel's
 board.

I saw the host,—a sodger bricht ; the famous fairmer
 chiel,

Hob-nob wi' oor 'fat fodgel wicht, the Knight o' Caulk
 and Keel.

Head held to head, I saw them pore on some rare
 pictur'd page,

And set the table in a roar wi' comments saut and sage.

Hoo lang I wander'd in the Past is yet to me unknown,

But Sleep her robe had o'er me cast ere half the nicht
 had flown ;

And O the glorious glints and gleams revealed to Fancy's
 sicht,

As through the witchin' land o' dreams she waved her
    fairy licht !

I hear the Laird his wit ootpoor on bygane deeds and
    times,

And hear the hero o' the hoor rehearse his latest rhymes ;

And, tho' the pipes and bottles shak' at Grose's least
    guffaws,

I trow he's neither sweir nor slack to gie the lines
    applause.

Anon they fret and fume and fuss o'er some historic
    lees ;—

But Fate (alas, 'twas ever thus !) a change o' scene
    decrees:

Just as the antiquarians big began a gran' debate

I wauken'd up to hear a gig come birlin' to my gate ;

And hardly had the echoin' street gi'en place to peace
    aince mair

When step by step twa pair o' feet cam' trampin' up the
    stair ;

I hear a hand for entrance ca' ; the knob roun' half-way
  turns,
Wide swings the door against the wa', and in strides—
  ROBERT BURNS !

As on the bed his plaid he coost I kent the Poet weel
Frae mony a portrait reproduced in stooka, stane and
  steel.

Anither bard made up the twae, and nae unwelcome guest,
Rare SANDY WILSON in his day to Burns the second best !
Upon his back he bore a gun ; birds frae his belt hung
  doun ;
Columbia's, Caledonia's son that sleeps in Penn's auld
  toun !

The strangers e'ed me for a while, and ne'er a word we
  spak'
Till Burns stapt forrit wi' a smile, and thus begoud the
  crack :—

" Fear not my friend ! for naething wrang my trip to you
    shall bode ;

And Wilson here,—he cam' alang as kennin' best the
    road !

We aft hae watched ye at your wark, and pleased to see
    the same, .

A score o' times we've made remark, ' Some nicht we'll
    seek his hame ; '

And so to send a sign before, last week we gave decree

That you should licht upon the lore that was so dear to
    me.

Here's Francie's auld familiar text ; shortsyne I left
    himsel'

Collectin' data for his next, ' Antiquities o'—well,

We'll tak' oor seats."——

Says Wilson : " Ay
        What Rabbie says is true ;

A towmond back I'll nae deny this trip we've had in
    view.

I've seen you scan my youthfu' lays that Fate has failed
to kill,

And heard the hinnied words o' praise ye pass'd upon
my skill;

And when I saw you come yestreen, by ruth and rev'rence
led,

And drap a tear upon the stane that shields my narrow
bed,

In flesh and bluid aince mair array'd I voo'd to leave my
biel'

And thank you for the love display'd that only bards can
feel."——

Here Burns took up the ancient tome, and restin't on
his knee :

" Nae mair to Romans was their Rome than this auld
work to me !

I mind, as thro' the leaves I look, my greatest, grandest
lay,

Burns. Betwixt the brods o' this braw beuk first saw the licht o'
day !

Here ' Tam o' Shanter ' cam' to life beside the banks o'
Ayr,

Alang wi' Kate the ' gentle ' wife his drinkin' tried sae
sair."—

Wilson. " An' ' Souter Johnny,' drouthy carle, here made his
maiden boo,

To stoyter henceforth thro' the warl' wi' swats and
whiskey fu'.

The cosey Ale-house ingle seat ; the landlord's laugh
sae clear ;

The maut-wife's favours, ' secret,' ' sweet,' were first
encounter'd here.

Here Usquebae, fiends couldna fleg, first hove upon our
sicht,

And here Tam's mere, immortal Meg, first took her
fearsome flicht ! "——

" The painfu' pairtin' at the inn, the keystane o' the
nicht,

The thunder's dread and dreary din, the lichtnin's
glancin' bricht;

Weird sichts the bauldest he'rts micht fear, alang the
turnpike lined,

In haunted howes and hillocks here first flashed upon
the mind.

Here first did dubs and darkness strive to stay my hero's
speed,

And wind connive wi' rain to rive the bonnet frae his
heid;

Here first the valiant Tammas saw the gleam amang the
trees,

And here the sacred biggin's wa' first burst into a
bleeze!"——

" Here first before the ruined pile, despisin' weet and
cauld,

Tam airtit Maggie thro' the stile, by Barleycorn made
bauld;

Wilson. Retauld in rhymes a thoosand times, here first fowk
cam' to learn
The gruesome sichts that thro' the lichts the twasome
could discern."——

Burns. " Deep dyed in gore, grim tools o' strife were ranged
aroun' the room—
Keen blades that snap the threads o' life before the pirns
are toom !
And dainteths there, e'en deils micht please, in ilka neuk
were stuck,
Frae tongues o' lawyers lined wi' lees, to priests' he'rts
black as muck." *——

Wilson. " On wrecks o' tables, strewn aboot, lay limbs frae young
and auld,
Enough to mak' the hair stan' oot an' gar the blood rin
cauld !

---

* To be found only in the *Grose* copy of " Tam o' Shanter."

Warlocks and witches in their mids, white corpses there *Wilson.*
   by croods,

In coffins black, withoot the lids, were standin' in their
   shroods !

Alang the wa's, in ghastly bands (while fairies dreel'd
   and danced),

They waved the blue lichts in their hands and stared
   like folk entranced !

Here Hornie in the winnock sole first burst upon our
   view,

And daur'd to show his visage droll as piper to the crew.

His pooer and pathos can we gauge, wha made the auld
   kirk dirl ?

E'en yet, whene'er we turn the page, we hear his chanter
   skirl !

We see him wale his choicest tunes, and launch them
   frae the laft,

Till wi' the magic o' his soun's the dancers a' gang daft :

Noo het and reekin' at their pranks the Kitties cast
   their claes,

Wilson.   And Nannie wi' the souple shanks her cuttie sark displays !

Aboon the loodest o' them a' we hear her yelp and yell—

But, mair than e'er the fairmer saw, we see brave Tam himsel' ;

We see him feast upon the splore till sicht and senses soom,

And hear him roar the bauld encore that signall'd forth his doom ! "——

Burns.   " The music stops ! the lichts gang oot ! our hero hameward wheels,

But barely gets his beast aboot, when whoop ! they're at his heels ;

Auld Cloots and a' his hellish crew, wi' Nanny in the lead—

Ah, Tam ! ah, Tam ! your Maggie noo maun show her utmost speed ! "—— ·

Wilson.   " O, sic a race and sic a rate nae mortal saw before,

And Time, its maister or its mate, shall witness nevermore !

Puir Tam ! His he'rt gangs duntin' sair at ilka splash *Wilson.*
and spang,

As swift the carlins cleave the air wi' horrid clash and
clang.

Skelp ! flee they on thro' sleet and slime, wi' mony a
tack and turn,

Nane gainin' time nor losin' time until they sicht the
burn,

When Nanny spurts for Tammie's pow, to flay him like
a pig,

And fleet as arrow frae the bow Meg bounds across the
brig !

Safe, by her hinmost dreadfu' jump, she brocht her rider
hale,

But only noo can cock a stump whaur aince she shook
a tail,

For Nannie, sweir to sacrifice baith Tam and Nick's
esteem,

Claught Maggie's besom in her vice afore she cross'd the
stream !

Wilson. And Tam ! He voos, as prood he dichts frae Meg the
flecks o' faem,

His spates and sprees on market nichts henceforth he'll
haud at hame !——

" Then shield the book frae crack, and crease, nor seek
your praise to stint,

For here our Maister's maister-piece first saw the licht o'
print ! "——

Burns. " And never while oor hamely Scotch is read in verse or
prose

May cauld Oblivion drive his coach across the realms o'
Grose ! "——

At this, by some unchancie means, my lamp began to
gloom,

I raised my head to find my frien's had vanished frae
the room,

I heard a soond like muffled drums and pibrochs in the
air,

And lookin' oot, aboon the lums that line the Delaware,

I saw a fleece o' gowden fire gang trailin' o'er the toun,

And by the auld Swedes' Chapel spire * a siller star drap
doun !

Syne up the howe, like funeral knells, resoundin' in a
raw,

North Camden's drowsy clocks and bells proclaimed the
hour o' twa ;

But o'er the Jersey meadows green the fiery dawn had
sped

Ere, musing on the midnicht scene, I creepit to my bed !

---

* Wilson is buried in the Old Swedes' Churchyard, Philadelphia.

EPISTLE TO JOHN SHEDDEN.

(On receiving a kindly letter anent the foregoing poem.)

DEAR FRIEN',—I'll mak' nae lang palaiver
Or seek to deave ye wi' a haver
O' sweetly clinkit clish-ma-claiver,
    To show my airt,
But thank you for your gracious favor
    Wi' a' my he'rt !

Yet, man, your style ye put sic viv in,
I tak' your praise wi' some misgivin';
To gie a Rhymer when he's livin'
    Sae heich a waft,
An' me—that's hardly got my niv in,
    Ye maun be daft !

Since Time began, whate'er the cause,

It's fix'd as ane o' Nature's laws

To stint the Poet o' applause

      As weel as bread,

Until he fills the maggot's maws

      Amang the dead !

And when he's fairly o'er the burn

Withoot the sma'est chance to turn,

There's coontless thoosan's gleg to mourn

      The clever cheil,

And big a costly Vase or Urn

      Aboon his biel' !

Were gifted Mac.,* your busy frien'

That rules Instruction's fair demesne,

---

* Dr. James MacAlister, now President of Drexel Institute—then
Superintendent of Education, Philadelphia.

Wi' jist ae half your kindly een

To view my Lay,

I'd face the warl wi' face serene

For mony a day.

I think mysel' (conceit, I'se warran'!)

The Piece, tho' maybe something daurin',

An' here an' there thro' fau'ties glaurin'

Some oot o' joint,

Is nae jist a'thegither barren

O' pith and point !

O, man, to spen' a week at hame

In that dear land I needna name,

Whaur first I woo'd wi' rustic fame

The Doric Muse,

Three times the wealth that I can claim

I'd nae refuse !

I then inspired by scenes sublime

Micht gie ye something worth your time,

But in this foreign prosy clime

    I maist despair

To get my Fancy workin' prime

    Forever mair !

Dame Fortune's but a spitefu' witch

To dird a fallow in the ditch,

And syne for fear he may get rich

    Ev'n howkin' there,

Infect him wi' the poet's itch

    To keep him bare !

Could I but wander at my swing

Withoot a thocht but live and sing,

Oor mither tongue ance mair would ring

    To lands remote ;

But warldly cares—they clog the wing,

    And cramp the note !

5

Yet never mind ！　Tho' poortith's stang

Eenoo may cause an antrin pang,

Mair fruitfu' days may come or lang

　　　To creesh my han',

And I, content, will lilt my sang

　　　Until they dawn !

SONG—THE BONNY LASS BEYOND THE SEA.

SHE's far awa', the lass I lo'e,

   Across the wild Atlantic's faem ;

Nae Scotia but Columbia noo

   The fairest o' the fair can claim :

   O, Fortune sairly is to blame

Sic cruel fate to fa' to me,

   By poortith doom'd to mourn at hame

The bonny lass ayont the sea !

As dowff I daunder by the burn

   Whaur aft we met, but noo nae mair,

Aye thinkin' whan will she return

   Hope fa's nae fit to fecht despair !

   Like ghaists they haunt me late an' ear',

The dreary days I still maun dree,

The ragin' waves she yet maun dare,

The bonny lass ayont the sea !

Wi' achin' he'rt I pass'd yestreen

Her father's steadin', and the ha'

That used to blink sae blythe an' bien

Look'd unco bare wi' her awa' :

Baith but an' ben as cauld as snaw

Without the glamourie o' her e'e,

The pride, the flow'r, the queen o' a',

The bonny lass ayont the sea !

Yon chiel that to the yokin' goes,

At set o' sun his labors cease ;

The gloamin' brings him sweet repose,

But nae for me sic blest release.

I waukrif' toyte frae bed to deece,

Till dawn has knockt the nicht ajee—

    She's spoilt my rest and wreckt my peace

The bonny lass ayont the sea !

   .   .   .   .

Ye Powers that feel for lovers leal,

    Afore wi' dool I fairly dee,

Bring back to bide by Bogieside

    The bonny lass beyond the sea !

EPISTLE TO W. E. GLADSTONE.

WHILE laith to gie her men and deeds
　A patriotic blaw,
Daft pride o' country sometimes leads
　A fool to get a fa'!

Shortsyne, in writin' to a frien'
　On Scotia's favor'd lot,
I had the impudence, I ween,
　To claim you as a Scot!
But lately, sir, the Southron clan
　Wi' greed are grown sae bauld,
They coont you as their countryman,
　Whilk gars the North look cauld!

Ye speak o' Caledonia stern
    Sae couthie and sae kind,
I've look'd upon you as her bairn
    Since ever I can mind.
Wha lives, I ask, can speak like you,
    Wi' sense and style sae grand,
On a' that loyal Scotsmen lo'e
    Wha camna frae the land
Whaur Bruce and Wallace drained their veins
    To richt the tyrant's wrangs,
Whaur Scott and Burns in hamely strains
    Pour'd oot immortal sangs?

But why the sad conclusion shun?
    Soon came the Cockney sneer:
"In England born the records run"—
    And I to own am sweir!
He's English born—tho' that be true,
    A Scotchman is he still,
His blood is ours and breedin' too,
    Or I hae tint my skill!

Hoo far I'm richt, an' wrang hoo far,

There's nae ane here can tell,

And hence I thocht I micht do waur

Than leave it to yoursel' ;

So gin ye find the time somehow

To put me oot o' pain,

Whatever wye ye redd the row

Your friend shall nae complain ! *

---

* See Appendix B.

TO A BURNS CONTEMPORARY OF
MY ACQUAINTANCE.

Come, here's my hand, auld Toddy Quech,
    Frae Tam o' Shanter's Inn at Ayr,
There's mony a chiel would puff and pech
    To mak' yoursel' his loving care,
And may the Quaker City Scot,
That winna toast ye, go to—pot!

O, gin we here could conjure up
    The Souter and his crony Tam,
And set them roun' this pewter cup,
    And watch them at their famous dram,
That had an end, to say the least,
That made immortal man and beast!

As in a dream we seem to see

  The kebbuck heel, the tappit hen,

And hear the landlord in his glee

  Awake the echoes but and ben ;

Altho' withoot the tempest rair'd,

Within they neither kent nor cared.

We see the Souter draw the bung

  And, hidlins, tak' the tither skyte

To weet his whistle, lowse his tongue,

  And moistify his gizzen'd kyte ;

And hear him, as he prees the maut,

Proclaim it fau'tless to a fau't !

We see Tam as he laughs and chats,

  Withoot a thocht o' Kate or hame,

And sips the barmy reamin' swats,

  And blaws awa' the froth and faem,

And hear him ring for mountain dew,

For ale gets wersh when fowk get fou !

But noo it's half a score o' howps,

    Whaur ane afore wad brawly sair,

 So jills lead on to mutchkin stoups,

    And mutchkin stoups to something mair ;

For only when the pig rins dry

They condescend to say Goodbye !

When thae rare worthies met to crack,

    And tauld their stories turn aboot,

Auld Mug ye sat, wi' humpy back,

    And drank in ilka word nae doot ;

Guid faith, ye noo micht raise a reek

Gin ye made up yer mind to speak !

Oor Poet voos he fand the Muse

    At times amang the barley-bree ;

Come tell's—Did Robbie Burns carouse

    In public howffs wi' sic as thee ?

Nay, Did he ever press his mou'

Against the very lips o' you ?

Did Holy Willie whyles drap in
  To fill his Tassie or his Horn,
And end by fillin' up his skin,
  And campin' in the ditch forlorn,
The whyle he sang wi' pious stress—
" *High is the rank we now possess* " ?

O, hoo we envy you sic nichts
  As when the Poet wad convene
Wi' Aiken, Gaun, and ither lichts,
  To drink the health o' Bonny Jean ;
And mix the glasses' clink at times
Wi' clink o' sweetly rinnin' rhymes !

Noo gane are a'—the daft, the douce,
  The rich, the poor, the guid, the ill—
But YOU ! weel primed wi' amber juice,
  As spruce and sprightly are ye still
As when the bard, beside your lug,
Drank inspiration frae the Jug !

Lang may ye come to circle roun'

 Amang the cronies centréd here,*

And link oor city wi' the toon

 To Scots and Scotland ever dear,

But dearest as the day returns

That dates the birth of Robert Burns !

---

* Read at the Eighth Annual Banquet of the Tam o' Shanter
Club of Philadelphia, 1891.

SONG—THE MILLER O' HIRN!

(To James Scott-Skinner, Composer of the Tune.)

THE fiddlin' Muse sae sweet an' braw,
 Tho' mony try to win her, O!
On nane her favors will bestaw
 Except a Scot ca'd Skinner, O!
Slee Jamie kent the wye to woo,
 And tho' she whyles wad girn, O,
His daring frae the lassie drew—
 The Miller o' the Hirn, O!

  Hech hey! the sweet strathspey,
   The lythesome, blythesome Hirn, O!
  Whate'er ye gie O play to me
   The Miller o' the Hirn, O!

It is an air micht move a saunt,
  Forbye a graceless sinner, O !
And bards o' gratitude are scant
  That wadna praise oor Skinner, O !
May joys come to him ilka day,
  Till he has toom'd life's pirn, O !
Lang may he live amang's to play
  The Miller o' the Hirn, O !

  Hich hey ! the grand strathspey,
    The slashin', dashin' Hirn, O !
  The fire o' Feugh is in its sough—
    The Miller o' the Hirn, O !

When first I heard the famous spring
  I liked its cheerin' binner, O !
And noo I wad gie onything
  To hear it play'd by Skinner, O !
Nae better lilt's upon the roun'
  To lichten labor's birn, O !

Care flees afore his glorious tune,
  The Miller o' the Hirn, O !

      Hoich hey ! the fine strathspey,
        The slidin', glidin' Hirn, O !
      I'd trudge a day to hear him play
        The Miller o' the Hirn, O !

Guid fiddlers noo are hard to get,
  And aye they're growin' thinner, O !
But ne'er will Caledonians fret
  As lang's we hae oor Skinner, O !
And for a strain we needna grane,
  We hinna far to kirn, O !
Afore we get ane o' his ain,
  The Miller o' the Hirn, O !

      Heech hey ! the bauld strathspey !
        Inspirin', firin' Hirn, O !
      It fills us thro', fair fiddlin' fu',—
        The Miller o' the Hirn, O !

Ye dons that deftly dirl the bow,

And you but raw beginners, O !

Steek nae a styme till ye ca' throw

This maister-piece o' Skinner's, O !

As lang's the raffy, royal Dee

Roars by the rock and fern, O !

Will Scotia's foremost Schottische be

The Miller o' the Hirn, O !

Hooch hey ! the rare strathspey,

The warmin', charmin' Hirn, O !

The pick an' wyle o' Britain's Isle,—

The Miller o' the Hirn, O !

A FEW WORDS TO WALT WHITMAN.

"Stranger, if you passing meet me, and desire to speak to me, why should you not speak to me?"

"And why should I not speak to you?"—W. W.

LANGSYNE, in far aff Aiberdeen,

I mind it jist as weel's yestreen,

The very day I set my een

Upon your book ;

And aye sin' syne I've bless'd the frien'

That made me look.

It took I own nae little while

Your ways and mine to reconcile,

But in the end ye could beguile

An evening fine ;

And noo your stuff, if nae your style,

I think divine !

Hale towmonds three hae jinkit roun'
Sin' hopes o' gear wi' witchin' soun'
Enticed me frae the Granite Toun
    On Scotia's shore,
And set me wi' a dirdum doun
    Beside your door !

And, man, it's odd, for a' oor tramps,
That you and I should pitch oor camps
In this dull land o' sand and swamps
    Whaur undevall'd
Malarial chills and colic cramps
    Rack young and auld !

To write you aft I've tried in vain,
And never mair I will maintain
Was humble rustic Poet fain
    Since time began,
But aye my hamely simple strain
    Held back my han'.

I maist had own'd my Musie cow'd,

Tho' sairly had the jaud been jow'd,

When chance into my clutches row'd

   An auld *Review*,*

And there I read a cunning strowd

   That cam' frae you.

It spak' o' Robin Burns frae Ayr—

My country's pride, beyond compare !—

Wi' sic appreciation rare

   In ilka pairt,

Frae that time onwards, I declare,

   I gather'd he'rt !

And, noo that I hae gane so far,

Tho' neither ribbon, rose nor star

---

* *North American Review* for Nov., 1886; " Robert Burns as Poet and Person," by Walt Whitman.

Frae Empress, Kaiser, King or Czar

  My breast bedecks,

To you—a brither bard—I daur

  To pay respec's !

Let ithers wait till ye gang hence

Afore they sing your Wit and Sense,

I sanna swither to dispense

  My tribute noo,

And hope ye winna tak' offence

  At what's your due !

When first your Lay went o'er the Water

I trow it raised an unco' clatter,

And few there were inclined to flatter

  We must confess,

While some declared you were a Satyr,

  And naething less !

Ev'n here, at hame, it was decreed

Sic strains could only weel proceed

Frae some half-filled or jummelt heid,
　　An', faith, for lang
They tried their best by stint o' breid
　　　To check your sang !

But Age cam' in wi' kindly frost,
And as in peace your taes you toast,
Frae Jersey to the Western Coast
　　　Nae ither name
Can a' Columbia's annals boast
　　　　To match your fame !

Lang may you live unscaithed by care
Beside the queenly Delaware,
And a' your days bring rowth o' fare
　　　As past they flie ;
Syne at the finish may ye share
　　　The Life on Hie,
Amang the Stars that nevermair
　　　Can dwine or die !

SONG—JOHNNY YET!

I'VE traivell'd in my time afar,
 But never met wi' ony
That I would tak', for good for waur,
 Afore my mannie, Johnny!

Tho' weel I lo'e oor bairnies braw,
 And we've had bairnies mony,
I lo'e himsel' abune them a'—
 He's first and best, my Johnny!

As Life's lang road we've warslt doon,
 Thro' smooth and stiff and stony,
So far he's brocht me safe an' soun',
 And still I'll trust my Johnny!

Altho' to you he's bald and bow'd,

 To me he's blythe and bonny,

And since my he'rt he firstlin's jow'd

 I've met wi' nane like Johnny !

There's gowd on merrie England's shore,

 And gear in Caledonie,

But I would spurn it three times o'er

 Than live withoot my Johnny !

Tho' Death, I hope, may spare us lang,

 When doon he cuts my crony,

Where'er the laddie has to gang

 I'll share his fate, my Johnny !

WORLD'S FAIR SCOTTISH GAMES.

In '93 the fun we'll see
    Needs nae great *Exposition*,
Gin half the plans in clever han's
    Should ever reach fruition ;
For then we'll view in coontless droves
    The cultured and the raw go
Frae oot their native glens and groves
    To rally in Chicago !

O, wha need try to lichtlify
    The Exhibition's greatness,
Or seek to hint there's ocht that's in't
    That's typical o' blateness ?

Some fain would hurt wha can but hiss,

So jouk and let their jaw go,—

There hae been lots o' Fairs ere this,

But only ae Chicago !

Frae far and near upon our sphere

Doun to the least iota

Nae bit o' grun' that greets the sun

Will fail to send its quota.

We'll see the doctor and divine,

The learnéd in the law go,

And mony a ane o' humbler kin'

Assemble in Chicago !

There will be Kings and sic like things

Nae doot amang the ferlies,

And Dukes and Lords wi' stars and swords,

And Marquises and Earlies :

But come they when they like, say I,—
　Let Sultan or let Shah go,
I question if they rate as high
　As mony in Chicago!

There INDUSTRY will vie with ART
　To show our planet's glories,
And SCIENCE too will play her part
　And tell her wondrous stories!
But nane o' a' thae sichts ava,
　Whaur bonny and whaur braw go,
Will match the squads o' kilted lads
　Competin' in Chicago!

Auld CALEDON strike up your drone
　And bid the Clansmen muster,
And pity tak' the senseless pack
　That tries to dim your lustre!

Unconquer'd yet for brawn or brain,
    Frae Cottage or frae Ha' go,
We'll trust ye still to haud your ain
    At hame or in Chicago!

Wae worth the sour and sulky boor
    Wha wadna cross the ocean
To see the GAMES Columbia claims
    Will ding the wildest notion!
Whaur those wha seek the Scot to fash
    Will in the stirkie's sta' go,
And ilka nerve be strained to smash
    The records at Chicago!

O Land o' Cakes, the Toun o' Lakes *
    Wi' you will nae be sparin',
Ye'll nae gae wrang whaure'er ye gang
    But meet wi' royal fairin'!

---

* The Modern Venice.

The Highland boys of Illinois

Will watch you till your wa' go,

And gi'e ye joy without alloy

As lang's ye're in Chicago !

Then here's good luck to Scotland's week

And a' that then forgaither,

And may our Patron Saint bespeak

Good health and pleasant weather !

For SCOTIA's sons throughout the world

In '93 will a' go

To see the LION FLAG unfurled

Wi' honours in CHICAGO !

NURSERY SONG—THE BOWGIE O' THE LUM.

My bairnies, noo, it's time for bed; guid-nicht to dinsome play;
Come roun' my knee and rest yoursel's, you've rompit a'
the day;
Frae morn to noon and noon to nicht, thro' sunshine
and thro' rain,
Your steer is like to fell the hoose and turn my very
brain;
While sings the kettle on the crook to pussy's cheerfu'
thrum,
I'll tell you o' a little man, the Bowgie o' the Lum!

Tho' hardly bigger than the ba' ye bounce upon the
green,
He has a score o' cockin' lugs an' half a hunner een!

And owre his humpy-dumpy back hangs—danglin' like
a tail—

A sooty pock sae braid an' lang that it could haud a
whale !

Ye wadna seek twa sichts o' him for ane wad mak' ye
dumb,

Ae blink o' this wee mannikie, the Bowgie o' the Lum !

A' day he doses in his hame amang the curlin' reek,

I've seen his den when lookin' whyles whaur young folk
maunna keek ;

But when the mirk begins to fa' and grass to kep the dew

He sprachles doon to look aboot for little weans like you !

When bairns are sweir to gang to bed—ah, then he's
sure to come,

The little wee bit mannikie, the Bowgie o' the Lum !

He jouks aboot the ingle-side, and glowers at young and
auld ;

And tho' he's but a little mite he's like a lion bauld !

He'll hae ye whistlin' thro' the air afore ye weel could
    wink,

And tak' ye to a cauldrif biel' wi' neither meat nor
    drink;

· The nicht he's prowlin' thro' the toun, short-syne I
    heard his hum,

The jinkin', jumpin' mannikie, the Bowgie o' the Lum!

When pillow'd heads the Bowgie sees, he to his hame
    will creep—

He maunna crook a scratty paw on bairns that want to
    sleep;

But greetin' geets he'll rin to meet frae miles ayont the
    moon,

And woe betide the waukrif' wean that winna cuddle
    doon!

Eenoo, impatient for a trip, I hear him beat his drum;

Then tak' your choice—a cosy cot, or Bowgie and the
    Lum!

EPISTLE TO "LA TESTE."

" Stand still, true POET that you are !
  I know you ; let me try and draw you.
Some night you'll fail us ; when afar
  You rise, remember one man saw you—
Knew you—and named a STAR !"—BROWNING.

———

HAIL, wise and witty WILLIE LA,
  Lane Lav'rock o' the North !
Good luck was wi' the tenty twa
  That sent your volume forth.
It fairly cam' withoot a flaw
  For a' the jump gigantic
  Across the wild Atlantic
To me sae far awa' !

7

O, rarely fand I sic a feast
   Betwixt a beukie's brods ;
For weel ye ken—sin' RAB's deceast—
   The Scottish Homer nods
Aye twa three dizzen lines at least
    For ane that's worth the printin',
    The Doric Musie stintin'
The Heliconian yeast !

But Laureate o' the Lossie's banks,
   She's been nae skimp wi' you !
Frae preface doon to final blanks,
   Your pen's been fill'd sae fu'
O' gritty quips and witty cranks,
    O' prose she maun hae stript it,
    And in Castalia dipt it,—
For which my grateful thanks !

Come Critic wi' the cankert phiz,
   Fish oot your fiercest fire !

Here bides a Bard that caresna biz
  For a' the help ye hire,
To prove those random rhymes o' his
  Are but a lot o' claivers ;—
  He weel can hear your havers
Whose work immortal is !

My fegs ! he would be hard to please,
  The coof who still would carp,
When in your horny hand you seize
  Auld Scotia's rustic harp !
Sae *tastily* ye touch the keys,
  And aye sae leal and lo'esome,
  Wi' sparks frae Nature's bosom
Your book is fair ableeze !

Nae thing to sing your genius spurns,
  Betwixt Time's head and heels,
Frae *A. B. C.'s* and *Butter Churns*
  To *Deities* and *Deils !*

Name ocht : ye tak' a twa three turns,
　　And syne set to the spinnin',
　　The rhymes as ready rinnin'
As e'er frae Robbie Burns !

Tho' nae court-laurels deck your broo,
　　Nor court-wines mak' ye keen,
Nae Tennyson can match, I troo,
　　Your lyrics *to the* QUEEN *!*
The words come slidin' frae your mou'
　　Sae lovin' and sae loyal,
　　High Chanter o' Chants-Royal
O'er a' the lave are you !

For those wi' he'rts as hard as stane,
　　There's pathos saft as Hood's,
Inwoven in your *Cripple Wean,*
　　On her *Amang the Cloods.*

The May-Rose in the Kirk-yard Green,—

The Midnicht Moonlicht Musin's,

Will nae need twa perusin's,

To draw tears to the een !

And wha can hit the Wit ye pit

Into your droll-like *Dreams,*

Or beat the Fancies ye gar flit

Thro' *Schedules* and sic themes ?

And when your Muse on Skinner-fit,

Sae spruce, sae spry gangs prancin',

Wha, tho' nae don at dancin',

Sae sulky as to sit ?

Your *Fine Arts play* I own is great,

And grand is *Craigen's Kiln !*

And rich the wye ye castigate,

The Saints o' Bishopmill !

And wow ! the words that twist and plait,
Thro' *Floater Allan* flashin',
O'er howes and hillocks dashin'
Like Spey when in a spate !

Let some licht-lovin' Bible bore,
Wha still moves in the mirk,
Glance thro' your *Odes*, and he'll deplore,
Ye dinna laird a kirk !
For sinners noo may sleep an' snore
Frae Bell to Benediction ;—
But nae sic dereliction
Should you lat lowss your lore !

Nae Reverend clad in coal-black coat,
For a' his hoasts and hems,
Can mate the cunning hand that wrote
Sic paraphrastic gems

As—titles o' but twa to quote—
Christ, Jairus' Dochter Raisin',
Or Eve, Lost Lassie, gazin'
At what her bite had brought !

O, sweetly sing ye a' the year
    Thro' pleasure and thro' pain ;
But keenest lugs we cock to hear
    When Love inspires the strain !
Nae poet lives your lays can peer,
    When courtin' coosh and canny,
    Some Nellie or some Nanny,
The dearest o' the dear !

But hoots ! mair headin's why rehearse ?
    Thro' a' your sapience shines ;
In *Sang* as in *Memoriam Verse*
    Or vaunty *Valentines !*

And tho' some may your name asperse

   For *Barley-bree Orations,*

   Your *Templar Exhortations*

Are neither scant nor scarce !

Elgina ! gin ye think to thrive,

   Tak' warnin' frae Dumfries !

Help WILLIE noo, while he's alive,

   Or henceforth haud your peace !

For just as sure as four's nae five,

   Till Albion's back be broken,

   While Scotch is spell'd or spoken,

His stanzas shall survive !

Nae langer his deserts adjourn,

   An' heap shame on your heid,

By raisin' Obelisk or Urn

   For TESTER when he's deid !

Let Time ne'er say ye loot him mourn

    For bannock in his bossie

    That sang so sweet by Lossie,

Moravia's bonny burn !

But lang may Death defer his claim

    On you, blythe-hearted WILL ;

Yea, may he knòck your Gallic name

    Clean frae his list until

I live as lang as Laing * whose fame

    Has e'en been wafted hither ;

    Syne hand and hand thegither

Content we'll hobble hame !

And, dootless, when we cast oor clay,.

    And seraphs stand complete,

---

* The reputed Elgin Centenarian.

Ye'll find auld scenes we may survey
    Frae some saft cosey seat,
Near-by the glorious Scots wha hae
    Got their reward before us,
    To sing wi' them in chorus
Forever and for aye !

SONG—THE LASS I LO'E SAE DEARLY, O!

WHAUR Dev'ron winds thro' meadows sweet,
　When moon and stars shine clearly, O!
I wend my way wi' joy to meet
　The Lassie I lo'e dearly, O!

The wind blaws saftly in my face,
　And a' thing aye looks cheerly O!
When I haud for the trystin' place
　To her I lo'e sae dearly, O!

Some ither maids I've seen ca'd braw
　That had but beauty merely, O!
She has been blest aboon them a'
　The Lassie I lo'e dearly, O!

I ken that she's a spotless flow'r,

   And trusts me richt sincerely, O !

There's naething ill shall e'er come owre

   The Lass I lo'e sae dearly, O !

Tho' Fortune's whip may lash me sair,

   And cut my hopes severely, O !

Gie me but her,—I'll seek nae mair,—

   The Lass I lo'e sae dearly, O !

BURNS—1892.

WHILE o'er the earth at festal boards to-night
  The glasses clink in memory of Burns,
  Beyond the Statues and the Sculptur'd Urns,
To dark Dumfries my fancy wings its flight ;
And Time reveals in retrospective light
  A drudging gauger with the poor returns,
  The slights, the sorrows, and the heartless spurns
That seared his soul and dimm'd his genius bright !

His richer friends look'd kindly on his rhyme,
But in his face they shut Preferment's gate ;
  And yet for all I shall be bold to say :
Sweet singing bird—he lived before his time,
But I believe he shared a better fate
  Than he would meet with if he came to-day !

January 25th.

SONG—THE AULD BOW-BRIG.

O, THE warl' looks braw an' bonny
   To a laddie at the school,
For the pleasant spots are mony,
   And the days unmix'd wi' dool :
I was then as blythe a chappie
   As a bird upon the twig,
And thocht life supremely happy
   By the Auld Bow-Brig !

It was fun beyond the matchin',
   Frae the gurglin' burnie's side,
Little troots an' minnies watchin'
   As they play'd at seek an' hide ;
And for 'oors we'd sit an' puddle
   Till the binner o' a gig,

Sent us aff like sheep to huddle
  'Neath the Auld Bow-Brig !

Tho' oor backs we had to double,
  And oor legs we had to pairt,
We got paid for a' oor trouble
  In the crossin' o' a cairt ;
And oor feet they wadna sattle,
  But for joy would dance a jig,
When the four-wheel'd 'bus would rattle
  Owre the Auld Bow-Brig !

• Growin' aulder in the day-time,
  It was aft oor stampin' grun',
Tho' it drew us near at nae time
  Like the aifter-supper fun :
By the unpretentious *Packet*
  I've had mony a rantin' rig,
And mony a merry racket
  By the Auld Bow-Brig !

But 'twas sweetest in the gloamin',

   When the days were warm an' lang,

Wi' a lassie to gang roamin'

   Whaur the water sung its sang ;

Ev'n the Laird o' Clova's treasures,

   They were held nae worth a fig,

When put up against the pleasures

   By the Auld Bow-Brig !

Noo the sea's betwixt us roarin',

   And has been for mony a year,

But in dreams I'm aften soarin'

   To the scenes I lo'e sae dear ;

And I'll never seek to grum'le,

   Be my fortune sma' or big,

While my he'rt can catch the rum'le

   Frae the Auld Bow-Brig !

IN MEMORIAM—JOHN SHEDDEN.

I DID not know him in his fiery prime
  But in the golden gloaming of his days,
  And all in vain my halting muse essays
To sum his virtues in my feeble rhyme.
A Scotchman first and last and all the time
  He never wearied in his words of praise
  For Caledonia and her deathless lays,
Tho' long an exile from his native clime.

His head was keen, his heart of purest ore,
  His hand unsullied in the storm and strife,
    But ever ready at Oppression's cry :—
Farewell, old friend ! Tho' here we'll meet no more,
  With those who felt the influence of your life
    While memory lives your name can never die !

8

AT THE LAYING OF THE CORNER-STONE, NEW CALEDONIAN CLUB HALL, OF PHILADELPHIA, U.S.A.

(Read by the Rev. A. Alison, D.D.) *

Four hundred years have come and gone,
    Since brave Columbus from the shores
Of our Old World, by pushing on,
    Flung wide a New World's doors.

And while throughout our hemisphere,
    The people all their homage pay,
We Scots have special reason here
    To celebrate the day.

---

* On Oct. 19, '92, 400th Anniversary of the Landing of Columbus.

With modern needs to keep in pace,
    From house to house no more to roam,
At last we've found a resting-place,
    A spot to call our home !

We leave the past without regret,
    And climbing up to greater heights,
To-day our Corner-Stone we set,
    And trim afresh our lights.

Now very soon to cheer our eyes,
    In grander style than we have known,
A Caledonian Hall shall rise,
    That we'll be proud to own.

Here in this cosy, snug retreat,
    Thro' summer's sun and winter's snaw,
May Scotsmen brither Scotsmen meet
    To whyle an 'oor awa'.

The auld may here at their command,
  Hae nichts to mak' them young again,
And youth will find that we hae plann'd,
  For brawn as weel as brain !

Henceforth may ilka member strive
  To keep dissensions from our gate,
That more than ever we may thrive
  In all that's good and great.

Columbia treats her strangers weel,
  The langer kent she grows mair dear,
And aff the heath nae Scot can feel
  So much at hame as here !

Pure mirth may dance while music pipes,
  Until they rock the biggin's wa's,
But temper wi' the Stars and Stripes,
  The Rampant Lion's paws !

To-day four hundred years ago,
 With booming guns and flags unfurl'd,
Columbus, as the records show,
 First landed on our world.

Like him our luck we sought to force,
 And left old barriers far behind,
Expecting on our Western course
 A better sphere to find.

Lo, Fortune has proved kind indeed,
 And starting from this favor'd date,
A Golden Era shall succeed
 The structure we create !

Long may we meet, a grateful band,
 To bless the fates that cheer'd our way,
And brought us to our Promised Land.
 Upon Columbus Day !

CRADLE SONG—HUSHIE BA-LOO!

Hushie ba-loo, my bairnie,
Lay your headie doun,
Steek baith your een and look to nane
O' a' thae things aroun'.
I'll hap your handies owre again,
Syne kiss your hinny mou',
Then lang an' deep, O may ye sleep,
Hushie ba, my bairnie,
Hushie ba-loo !

Hushie ba-loo, my lammie,
Noo ye maunna greet,
Or Mam may tak' her cuddles back
And put ye in the street.

Na, peace be here ! sic threats need fear
Nae diltit dear like you—
Hushie ba, my bairnie,
Hushie ba-loo !

Hushie ba-loo, my pettie,
Lo ! he's fa'n awa' !
Aboon his plaid ae hand is laid
As white as drifted snaw.
His cheeks are twa wee roses red,
And owre his shinin' broo,
Like rings o' gowd the curls are row'd—
Hushie ba, my bairnie,
Hushie ba-loo !

Hushie ba-loo, my troutie,
See his facie beams !
His poutin' mou' is pairted noo,
He's lauchin' in his dreams !

O, wha could miss sic honey'd bliss,

  As this ripe kiss to pu'?

Hushie ba, my bairnie,

  Hushie ba-loo !

Hushie ba-loo, my birdie,

  Cosy as a king,

My little doo is nestled noo,

  On slumber's silky wing.

The rhythm o' his balmy breath,

  Like music thrills me thro',

As calm and fair he dozes there—

  Hushie ba, my bairnie,

    Hushie ba-loo !

Hushie ba-loo, my laddie,

  Prince o' babies a',

I dinna speir that rowth o' gear

  May to your portion fa' ;

But when a man aye may⁻ye stan'

    Amang the good and true,

Hushie ba-loo, my bairnie,

    'Hushie ba-loo!

ABOOT OOR DOG.

(Not an Allegory.)

SAX year or mair we'd keepit hoose,
　A couple weel contentit,
And nae a man nor wife mair douce
　A dwallin' ever rented ;
When ae nicht sittin' roun' the log
　My Nannie put the query :
" What wad ye say to get a dog
　Like ither fowk, my dearie ? "

" A Dog," says I, " gin sae ye like
　Set oot the morn and buy him,
For me—I wadna hae a tyke,
　Nor for a mint be nigh him ;

They're a' the same frae whelp to cur,

    Tormentors sent to deave us,

And when they're straikt against the fur

    Aye ettlin' to mischieve us ! "

" Hoots, Jamie man ! " quo' Nannie syne,

    " Ye're grown an awfu' bigot,

But I've made up for aince my min',

    So jist shut aff yer spigot !

A Dog's a handy thing to hae

    Aroun' a body's ingle,

A helpfu' beast—a cheery ray

    To mairriet life or single ! "

" Jist think," my better half declared,

    " Hoo bolts and bars are bursted,

But wi' a tyke the hoose to gaird,

    The warst o' thieves are worsted !

And then as kind as ony cat,

    That gambols wi' her kittlins

He'll never let a crook or scrat
   Befa' oor bonny littlins ! "

I saw 'twas useless mair to speak,
   When Nannie was inclined to't,
We'd hae a dog afore a week,
   I had made up my mind to't.
And neist day to the toun she went,
   As I'm a true believer,
And half her simmer's savin's spent
   Upon a big retriever !

At least that's what the seller said,
   As Nanny catcht his jargon,
And in a blink the price was paid
   That nane micht rue the bargain.
Syne in an hoor the simple dame
   By Mr. Dog attendit,
As prood as Punch cam' mairchin' hame,
   And a' oor peace was endit !

He was a kin'ly lookin' brute,

    But looks are sair misleadin',

And in the hoose withoot a doobt

    He soon display'd his breedin'!

At denner-time the fun began,

    When " Tory " as they ca'd him,

· Dung in the fire the fryin' pan,

    And to the door I shaw'd him !

Up Nannie flichtert like a low,

    " Come, Jamie, man hae patience ;

Reflect afore ye raise a row

    Upon the beast's temptations.

He maun be wild for want o' meat,

    Sin' frae his hutch they haul'd him,

I'm nearly faintin' on my feet,

    And so I sanna scauld him ! "

So " Tory " was brocht in again

    Frae whaur the loons had chased him.

My lady claimed him as her ain,
  And in the neuk she placed him ;
And while she whined " puir Christian beast
  See hoo his herts a-quakin' ! "
He proved he was nae *Jew* at least
  By gobblin up the bacon !

He shoved his nose my chair beneath
  Defyin' me to steer him,
And aye he girned and bared his teeth
  When ony ane cam' near him :
Says I, " I'd like to see the day,
  A dog wad be my maister,"—
And sent him yelpin' frae my tae
  To look for stickin' plaister !

He made a dash straucht for the green,
  Whaur Nancy's wash was bleachin',
And tho' his lugs had timmer been,
  He must hae heard her screechin' ;

But never did he see the claes
　Until he lichtit on them,
And then he slacked his fleein' pace
　And danced a reel upon them !

He lunched upon a cloakin' deuk,
　And when he had secured them,
A brood o' chuckens neist he took
　And ane by ane devoored them ;
And naething done by halfs or thirds,
　But hale-wheel a'· thegither,
When he had dined upon the birds
　He supper'd on the mither !

We had a patch o' fancy flooers
　Aye kept in perfec' order,
But aifter " Tory " made his tours
　Aroun' the little border,
Ye couldna point a single spot
　That wasna snuffed and snowkit,

And ilka plant within the plot
  Up frae the root was howkit !

This nettled Nancy like mysel',
  She couldna stand it langer,
And wi' a maist unearthly yell
  She grabb'd him in her anger,
And tore him howlin' to the hoose,
  To bring him to his senses,
For he had play'd the very deuce
  Regairdless o' expenses !

Wi' help frae me—a task nae slim—
  She locked him in her chaumer,
An' wi' the door atween's an' him
  The air grew kin' o' calmer.
He whimpert for a whyle, 'tis true,
  As if we'd used him sairly,
But that died oot and ere we knew
  We had forgot him fairly !

Twa hours unkent had slippit by
  When frae the upper storey,
We heard a maist heart-piercin' cry
  That put's in mind o' " Tory ; "
An' rushin' up to learn the cause,
  In just a dizzen wordies :
We found a kist upon his paws,
  The bed upon his hurdies !

The scarlet fringes turned to threids,
  The lace to streamers strippit ;
The sheets and blankets torn to shreeds,
  The cheena crackt an' chippit :
O sic a mess the room was in
  When we had time to view it !
It lookt for a' the earth as gin
  A cyclone had swept thro' it !

My caip that held my heid as snug's
  It kept my pillow tidy,

9

Was twistit roun' twa sheepskin rugs
 And daidlt like a didy.
And Nancy maist gaed into fits,
 When lookin' roun' to don it,
She found the beast had chow'd to bits
 Her braw new Sunday bonnet !

Nicht cam' at last and found the dog
 Stretcht oot below the table,
A single step to styte or jog
 In truth he wasna able.
I venture't we micht lat him be,
 And only saw my blun'er,
When lichtnin' flashed frae Nannie's e'e,
 And she roared oot like thun'er :

" Hoo daur ye sic a thing presume !
 The fashious filthy snarler,
He sanna get the dinin'-room,
 He sanna get the parlor !

The kitchie's hingin' fu' o' meat,

    And for his like the sole hole

That I could ca' a safe retreat

    Is doon-stairs in the coal-hole ! "

" A wise solution lass," says I,

    " Your sense is maist amazin' ; "

And syne we baith began to try

    Wi' flinchin' and wi' phraisin'

To tryst him to the cellar-door,

    But never moved the crater,

And when I lowsed at him and swore

    It didna mend the maitter !

We baith got on oor thinkin' caips

    And tried to tempt the glutton,

By trailin' up an' doon the steps

    A greasy leg o' mutton ;

But no ! He had made up his min'

    His kyte nae mair to injure,

And tho' he whiles let oot a whine
   He never jee'd his ginger !

At last I liftit up a pail,
   Lip fou o' soapy water,
And ower the brute frae tap to tail
   I gart the slops play clatter !
It never brocht him to his feet,
   But in the splash and splutter,
I missed my balance, strained my queet
   And plumpit in the gutter !

Enraged at siccan feckless sport,
   I vood he'd be a croaker,
If I should swing next minute for't
   And warmin' up the poker,
I creepit up ahin' his Nibs
   That never had an equal,
Bored in the steel atween his ribs
   And waited for the sequel !

A yell !—a jump !—a rattlin' crash !
　　Glaiss chips aroond us sailin',
The kitchy window minus sash,
　　A slap made in the pailin' !
A pace that wadna shamed a tod
　　Or greyhound in his glory,
A whirl o' stew alang the road—
　　This was the last o' Tory !

But tho' the tyke kept on wi' fricht
　　Till we had fairly tint him,
Like Phoebus, when it sinks frae sicht,
　　His trail he left ahint him :
The Hoose frae front to back in spots
　　Was hobblin' o'er wi' vermin,
That took a week or mair an' lots
　　O' tyauvin' to extermine !

Since oor exploits wi' sic a rogue,
　　My wife's an alter'd woman,

She'll cross the street to dodge a dog

That seems her wye a-comin'!

And best o' a', which I micht ca'

The moral o' my story,

There's aye been peace between us twa

Sin we got rid o' Tory!

SONG—FOR A' THAT.

Tho' on our tracks misfortune noo
  May drive her wheel, and a' that,
A Scotsman true will never boo,
  Nor beg nor steal, for a' that !
  For a' that and a' that,
As in the past for a' that,
  Oor grun' we'll stan' wi' ony man
And bide the blast for a' that !

Tho' nae sae weel's we aince hae been,
  We'll nae lose he'rt for a' that ;
As lang as Scotland has a frien'
  We'll hae oor pairt for a' that !
  For a' that and a' that,
Tho' cairt may coup and a' that,

We'll try our micht to set it richt,
Nor tyne the houp for a' that !

The langest lane has got an en',—
   We'll breist the burn for a' that ;
Some bonny day afore we ken
   The tide will turn for a' that !
   For a' that and a' that,
Nae tearfu' e'e for a' that ;
   Times hae been waur than what they are,
We'll thankfu' be for a' that !

The mirkest nicht maun aye tak' flicht,
   The day aye daw' for a' that ;
Whaur shadows bide there maun be licht,
   What mortal never saw that !
   For a' that and a' that,
We'll sing oor sang for a' that ;
   Gin days be dour and fowk be sour
They'll change or lang for a' that !

A PARAPHRASE.

When ye hae look'd upon the lass
  Ye feel inclined to mak' your ain,
Some glarin' fau'ts ye may let pass,
  For Love beguiles the Lover's brain ;
So get some auld and practised hands
To tell you hoo your lady stands !

And syne when ye set oot to woo,
  Keep fu'some phrasin' frae your tongue :
Straucht-forrat speech will help ye thro',
  While lees will lose the auld or young :
Just say ye lo'e the lassie weel,
And she'll o'erlook your want o' skeel !

She'll maybe for a short time froon,

 And cut ye wi' a caulrif e'e,

But lang afore the nicht gang roun',

 She'll wish ye had the pluck to pree ;

And greet her lane an hoor or twa

If ye should fruitless wear awa' !

What tho' she mak' a feint to fecht,

 And scowl and scaul' when ye draw near ?

She kens her " Na " has little wecht,

 And tries to gar ye true she's sweir,

To grant ye what she wouldna gie,

Had ye nae been mair strang than she !

When better kent, bear wi' her wheems,

 And bidena back to lat her ken

Hoo great and grand are a' your schemes,

 Aboon the schemes o' common men ;

And hoo the gear is roun' ye row'd,

For nane are proof against the gowd !

Be to your aiths as true as steel,

    But in your deeds mak' little din,

And gin your dearie treat ye weel,

    Stick to her side thro' thick and thin ;

Yea should misfortune at her bite,

Be last to flee tho' she should flyte !

Men can dee naething mair than skim,

    The depth that in the women lies ;

  .   .   .   . *

    Aboot their wiles is jist as wise ;

For aft a jaud when she says " Nay,"

Will sulk if you should tak' it sae !

By this you'll maybe understand,

    Who read my rambling verses thro',

---

* This line I had perforce to trim !

The softer sex of every land

Have bodies, parts and passions too,

And like to feast upon the sweets,

.　.　.　.　.　.　.　.　*

But weesht ! I fear I've been owre bauld,

To tell sic secrets in my sang,

Some things had better nae be tauld,

Tho' what's the truth—Can it be wrang ?

Then with this hint I'll end my rhyme :

Be ye not blate when comes your time !

---

* Immodesty the verse completes !

BURNS'S COTTAGE.

WEE Cottage by the banks o' Doon,
   Your roof is laigh, your rooms are narrow,
But we may search the warl' aroun',
   And look for lang to get your marrow.
Mair honor'd are your rugged wa's,
   That thro' the years so steively stand,
Than a' the Castles, College Ha's,
   And Kirks in Scotia's classic land !

Here was the humble peasant born,
   Who took Dame Nature for his teacher,
And holding caste and creed in scorn,
   Became his country's greatest preacher :
Who ruled thro' Love and Wit by turns,
   And still is King of all his clan,
Our darling bard, rare Robert Burns—
   He taught the world A MAN'S A MAN !

SONG—THE BONNY LASS O' BON-ACCORD.

I JIST had dander'd owre frae Nigg,
    To spend a forenicht in the toun,
And got the length o' Union Brig
    As mirk begood to sattle doon :
At he'rt as happy as a lord,
    Nae care nor thocht o' care I knew,
Till the bonnie lass o' Bon-Accord
    Flash'd like a star upon my view !

A blonde as lissome as a saugh,
    Wi' grace and ease in ilka turn,
Her een like dew-draps, and her lauch
    Melodious as the ripplin' burn :

I'd spurn the Bank o' England's hoard,

 And mair than millionaire wad be,

Gin the bonnie lass o' Bon-Accord

 Would only say she'd gang wi' me !

I ken the East as weel's the West,

 And North and South I've aften been,

Auld Scotia's brawest and her best,

 In cot and castle I hae seen :

But frae the Tweed to Muir o' Ord,

 I tell ye gin ye care to ca',

The bonnie lass o' Bon-Accord

 I set her far aboon them a' !

Nae ane by bribes could I induce

 To gie to me the lassie's name ;

I neither kent the street nor hoose

 In which she lived and made her hame :

And tho' the city I explor'd

 Frae mou' o' Don clear doon to Dee,

The bonnie lass o' Bon-Accord

'Twas never mair my luck to see !

Let parsons gin it please them preach

On what we lost by Adam's fa' ;

In spite o' what the kirks may teach,

The Scriptur's and the creeds and a',

I say that Eden was restor'd

To mortals on the earth below,

By the bonnie lass o' Bon-Accord,

And ever is where she may go !

O cruel Fortune that forbade

My een to licht on her again,

But bless her for the blink I had,

Tho' it was pleasure mixed wi' pain !

While Recollection can afford

My heart a bygane dream to hae,

The bonnie lass o' Bon-Accord

Will haunt me till my deein' day !

TO "SURFACEMAN."

On a Postal Card.

DEAR FRIEN'—while swirlin' whirlin' drift
Cam' skirlin' birlin' frae the lift ;
While Borèas in the gloamin' grey
Had maist blawn oot the licht o' day ;
While whistlin' horns an' clangin' clocks
Loot lads an' lasses lowss in flocks,
A couthie note, that bore your name,
This nicht cam' to my hand and hame !

It mak's me mair than pleased to find
Ye tak' my verse sae unco' kind,
And think at least sae weel o' me
As send your thanks across the sea !

10

This lang I've had a high regard

For your creations as a bard,

And since we first becam' acquent

O, mony a happy hour I've spent,

In readin' o'er and o'er again

The sweet productions o' your pen !

Lang may your pipe be heard to soun'

Aboon the din o' Embro' toun :

Fash nae your heid, nor fyle your mooth

Wi' Sass'nach lingo o' the Sooth ;—

In prose it's dootless trig an' terse,

But nae the tongue for tunefu' verse,

So stick to Scots, whae'er may flee,

And ye shall live till Burns shall dee !

January 19, 1892.

BURNS IN ABERDEEN.

(Suggested by reading a newspaper account of the ceremonies and
speeches at the unveiling of the BURNS STATUE, Aberdeen,
September 15th, 1892).

FIVE score o' years and five years mair
   Hae in the drift o' Time been smor'd,
Since rhymin' Robbie Burns frae Ayr
   Stroll'd thro' the streets o' Bon-Accord !
'Twas Sunday Nicht he struck the toun
   Wi' Willie Nicoll in a coach,
An' sic a twasome, I'll be boun'
   Hae nae sinsyne made their approach ! *

---

* Sam Johnson, wi' the gifted gab, pass'd thro' wi' "Boz." nae
lang afore, but what were they to rustic Rab, for a' their lades o'
classic lore ?

In fact, unless when Shakespeare play'd
   His dramas in the Weigh-house Square,
Wi' muckle truth it may been said
   The match o' Burns was never there !

On Monday morn when he had slept
   And donn'd his duds and wash'd his face,
He frae his sober lodgin's crept
   To tak' a stoyter thro' the place.
Togg'd oot in flamin' buck-skin breeks,
   His top-boots reachin' near his knee,
The bloom o' health upon his cheeks,
   He was a decent chiel to see !
Nae coat and vest o' hamespun stuff
   That weel the fairmer micht hae sair'd,
But happ'd in skyrin' blue and buff
   He look'd as bigsy as a laird !
And like himsel' to hae a smack,
   Unlike the feck o' fowk he knew

He loot his hair hing doon his back
 Unpoother'd in a ribbon'd queue !
Fresh frae his triumphs in the Sooth,
 But aucht-an'-twenty at the maist,
The Granite City saw with truth
 The bard in a' wye at his best.
Then was the darling Prince of Rhyme,
 As can be gather'd frae his lays,
If ever, in his golden prime,
 And in the happiest of his days !

I fancy him wi' easy stride,
 Stravaigin' street an' lane an' close
As they were ranged on ilka side,
 Aroun' the muckle Market Cross.
Perchance he wander'd to the Links
 To watch the Ocean shorewards row,
Or spent an hoor in puin' pinks
 An' musin' in the Denburn Howe !

Sma' doot there is he saunter'd owre

　Balgownie's Brig an' Brig o' Dee,

And spent the time to tak' a glower

　Amang the fishers at the Quay.

I'll vooch he thocht it worth his while

　To see the Auld Cathedral's spires,

And Education's massive pile,

　The pride o' Scotia's Northern shires !

　　　　　　-:-

This much we frae his notes may glean,

　Altho' his trip was made wi' haste,

He saw some fowk in Aiberdeen

　He thocht was muckle to his taste.

There met he, as he does confess,

　Wi' Mr. Ross,—'a fallow fine',

And Marshall that wi' some success

　Had tried to woo the tuneful Nine !

Professor Gordon, too, he saw,

　And scannin' Robbie's notes we see

' Good-natured '—' jolly-looking '—twa
    Good traits that took the Poet's e'e.
There too he met, and relished weel,
    As frae his sketch we needna doobt,
A famous and facetious chiel,
    The foremost printer thereaboot.
On Chalmers' stair by chance he spak'
    To Bishop Skinner, son o' JOHN ;
Wow ! when thae twa begoud to crack,
    I fear the ithers a' stood yon' !
And last, but least I sanna say,
    Tho' Norlan' bards were far frae scarce ;
He met wi Shireffs in his day,
    The Sandy Pope o' Scottish verse. *

Whaur did he see so rare a set,
    In a' his wand'rin's in the North ?—

---

* I'm proud of all that then transpired, but here's what more
than puzzles me : the "Minstrel" Burns so much admired—Professor Beattie —where was he ?

I trow their match he never met,
　Ayont the waters o' the Forth !

It taksna much to conjure up
　These shadows, from the realm o' dreams,
And set them roun' a social cup,
　To chat upon their fav'rite themes.
See, Burns presidin' like a-lord,
　Blythe Nicoll at the table's fitt ;
The ithers, rank'd aroun' the board,
　As near their guests as they could sit.
Perhaps they sipp'd Devanha dew,
　A noted brand o' barley-bree ;
For whatna sowff could thraw his mou',
　Wi' Rob an' Willie there to pree ;
I wat they spent nae cauld harangues,
　On dry affairs o' Kirk or State ;
But crack'd aboot the auld Scots sangs,
　Till it was time to tak' the gate.

I fancy Burns felt much at hame,

    For it was in the near-by Mearns

From whence the poet's father came,

    And Granny Burness raised her bairns.

Nae far awa' his kin lived still,

    By Bervie's burnie's brattlin' tide,

And in the kirkyard near Knockhill

    His forbears sleepit side by side.

Yea mair: to Aberdonian frien's

    That had migrated doun to Ayr,*

He was indebted in his teens

    For books that brocht him muckle lear!

And Skinner's father, rev'rend John,

    Nae prentice at the Doric lyre,

The younger singer look'd upon,

    And claimed as his poetic sire!

" Gae bring to me a pint o' wine,

    I'll drink," said Burns, "before I go,

---

* The family of Dr. Paterson.

A service to the old divine
    Whose numbers so divinely flow ! ''
" O, Tullochgorum's my delight !—
    The best song Scotland ever saw ! "—
Thus did the raptur'd Robbie write,
    As if his ain were nocht ava !
And there that day to Skinner's son,
    The Ayrshire bard by word o' mou'
Confess'd nae sma' that he had done
    Was to the Linshart Poet due.
" My ' Maillie ' some think nae sae bad,
    Frae Skinner's ' Ewie ' sprang," said he,
Then shouted out " O, 'an I had
    The loon that did it ! " in his glee.
" O, had I met him face to face,
    And held his worthy hand in mine !
Why did I pass so near his place,
    And yet nae worship at his shrine ?
" But say when next ye send your news
    How much I rev'rence and esteem

And love his truly Scottish Muse,

    For in his skill he stands supreme !

" I'm noo collectin' in my roun's

    Auld samples of our minstrel lore,

And would be pleased for Sangs or Tunes

    Frae Skinner's stock to grace my store.

Tho' I may hae but little claim,

    I fain would like if ye'd insist

That he should kindly put my name

    Upon his correspondents' list."

Syne, for the Bishop, Burns wrote oot

    His quarters in Edina toun,

Whaur in a month or thereaboot

    Auld Skinner mailed a letter doun :

And this same rhymed epistle sent

    Burns styled, as doubtless he believed,

The best poetic compliment

    He ever in his life received.

Yea, in immortal prose enshrined
  We hae't laid doun frae his ain han'
As lang's he lived he aft repined
  He didna meet the Grand Old Man !

So much for "lazy" Aberdeen,
  When Burns was but the Bard o' Ayr,
And noo his worth is better seen
  The "lazy toun" keeps up its share.

" A lazy toun "—the crazy loon
  Wi' sic a fling to pass it by !—
I'm glad he just had scribbled doun :
  "We come to Aberdeen to LIE ! "

Lo, noo, the latest o' her feats
  She's raised his statue cast in bronze,
And may the neist to grace her streets
  Be nane but TULLOCHGORUM JOHN's !

IN MEMORIAM: "LA TESTE."

*A Sprig o' Heath frae Jersey's soil by way of Garland
for his Grave.*

" 'LA TESTE' is dead !" so comes the news
　　Across the wild Atlantic faem ;
The darling o' the Doric muse
　　Now slumbers in his hindmost hame !

And shall the Scottish Laureate gang
　　Unnoticed to the kirkyard's gloom
Withoot the tribute o' a sang
　　To deck his unpretentious tomb ?

Shall puddlers in Parnassus Well
　　Be laid with pomp beneath the sward,
And nane be found a note to swell
　　In honour o' the rustic bard ?

O, Willie was a clever chiel,
   And tho' his face I never saw,
I kent him, and I lo'ed him weel,
   And mourn him noo that he's awa'.

He had his fauts—an' I hae mine—
   And ye hae yours, whae'er ye be,
Ah, frien', wash oot the motes frae thine
   Afore ye fash your brither's e'e !

Equipp'd beyond his fellow men,
   For verse he had the happiest turn,
And words cam' ripplin' frae his pen
   Spontaneous as the Lossie burn !

Unlike maist poets noo in vogue
   Whose drift the mass in vain divines,
Nae dark conundrum-weighted fog
   Obscured the purport o' his lines !

Gie readers blest wi' lear and time
  A singer skilled in mystic airts,
I'm partial to the simple rhyme
  That works its way to hamely he'rts !

Implanted by the ingle neuk,
  Or stretched beneath a shady tree,
Enraptur'd o'er his bonny book
  I've seen the 'oors like minutes flee.

For honest fun he had a smile,
  And thrumm'd his heart in sweet accord,
But in his strong satiric style
  His stylus oft became a sword !

And he could weep with those who wept,
  Give solace to the wearied frame,
And sparks o' hope that long had slept
  His rousing words could fan to flame !

Nae care could chill his genial crack,

    Nae dunts frae fate his hand could stay,

The world grew sunnier when he spak',

    And merrier when he trilled his lay !

Tho' stranger to a cosy nest,

    Thro' summer's sun and winter's sleet,

The bird kept singing in his breast

    Until his heart had ceased to beat !

His voice shall wake the woods no more,

    And yet 'tis comfort now to feel

He sleeps, with all his wand'rings o'er,

    Amang the scenes he lo'ed sae weel !

And tho' his lyre be noo laid by,

    Unstopp'd shall ring the minstrel's strains,

He is not dead—He'll never die,

    While Scotland and her speech remains !

SONG—WHEN THE SUN'S GANE O'ER THE HILL.

O, THO' I were e'er sae weary,
　　And the tryst sae far awa',
　　　When the bonnie flooers are closin'
　　　　Lest the mirk micht do them ill,
I would meet you, Nancy, dearie,
　　By the brattlin' burnie's fa'
　　　In the gowden summer gloamin'
　　　　When the sun's gane o'er the hill !

When the birds hae hush'd their singin'
　　In the bosky woods and glens,
　　　Whaur the water fresh an' foamin'
　　　　Dances doun to kiss the mill,

A' my cares ahint me flingin',

   Wi' a joy there's few that kens,

      I would meet you in the gloamin'

         When the sun's gane o'er the hill !

When the herd wi' fitfa' canny

   Frae the moss drives hame his kye,

      E'er the little starnies, blinkin',

         O'er the land their radiance spill,

I would meet you, dearest Nannie,

   'Neath the smilin' rosy sky

      In the lang lang simmer gloamin'

         When the sun's gane o'er the hill !

Had I a' the grounds sae grassy

   That the Mossat wimples thro'—

      Had I a' the cattle roamin'

         Thro' the bonny fields at will,

I would gie them a', my lassie,

   And would think then nae anew

      But to meet you in the gloamin'

         When the sun's gane o'er the hill !

A DOMESTIC DUET.

(To be Sung in Character.)

Tammas and Tibbie (with a few neighbours) at their ain Fireside.

Tibbie.—O sic a man is Tibbie's man !
    Frae lowsin' time to yokin',
The spoon is hardly frae his han',
    When he sets to the smokin'.
I wish his twist was in the moon,
    His spleuchan in Malacca ;
I never saw anither loon
    Sae browdent on Tobacca.

Chorus.—Female contingent.

> Sneezin' an' hoastin', hoastin' an' sneezin',
>> Your dwallin' chokit fu' o' reek,
>> Frae door-step to the chimney cheek,
> I trow it's very teasin'!

Tammas.—O sic a wife is Tammie's wife!
> Save when her kyte she's stuffin',
Ilk waukin' meenit o' her life
> She's snortin' an' she's snuffin'.
Thro' weather cauld and weather het
> She beats a' competition,
I never yet her marrow met
> For gettin' redd o' sneeshin'.

Chorus.—Male contingent.

> Sneezin' an' hoastin', hoastin' an sneezin',
>> The lady that ye swore to lo'e,
>> Snuff barket roun' her nose an' mou',
> I wat it's far frae pleasin'!

Tibbie.—The inside o' his gab wi' soot,

    As smudgy as a tunnel ;

His thrapple wa's frae tap to root

    As black's an engine's funnel ;

Sook, sook, he gangs thro' foul an' fair,

    The perseverin' body,

To blaw his siller in the air

    Seems a' the crater's study.

Chorus.—Female contingent.

    Sneezin' an' hoastin', hoastin' an' sneezin',

      To hae the best in ilka room

      A' clortit owre wi' smiddy coom,

      I trow it's very teasin' !

Tammas.—To see her whyles beside the bench,

    Dish-washin' in progression ;

A dicht, an' syne anither pinch,

    It truly is refreshin'.

Drap, drap, owre a' in blotches big,

She sheds the gowden mixter;

'Twould turn the stammack o' a pig,

To sit an evenin' next her.

Chorus of Males.—

Sneezin' an' hoastin, hoastin' an' sneezin',

On ilka side, in ilka place;

Auldmeldrum* starin' in your face,

I wat it's far frae pleasin'!

Tibbie.—Afore I heed his ilka whim,

On *dottle* and on *logie;*

I swear I'll dook baith pipe an' him,

Heels owre the heid in Bogie.

I've seen a chiel could tak' a puff,

And exerceese forbearin';

Tam keeps for ever at the stuff,

An' kensna what's a sairin'.

---

* A famous brand.

Female Chorus.—

> Sneezin' an' hoastin', hoastin' an' sneezin',
>
> The parlour stourin' like a mill;
>
> The kitchie smorin' like a kiln,
>
> I trow it's very teasin'!

Tammas.—Noo, Tibbie, lass, it's time to stay,

> Oor gabbin' and oor girnin';

We'll never mak' a brichter day,

> For ither's failin's kirnin'.

And brawly, brawly do ye ken,

> For a' my fiddle-faidle;

I'd sooner see ye wield the *pen*,

> Than steer the toddy-ladle.

Chorus, All.—

> Freezin' an' fiercely, fiercely an' freezin',
>
> The wintry-laden breezes blaw;
>
> But what care we for wind and snaw,
>
> Aroun' the ingle bleezin'!

Tibbie.—Ay, Tam, an antrin tilt nae doot,

 Is guid aneuch in sizzen ;

But in continwal castin' oot,

 There's neither rhyme nor rizzen.

So dinna tak' my haivers ill,

 Tho' whyles I mak a splutter ;

I'd raither hae ye toom an' fill,

 The *cuttie* than the *cutter !*

Chorus, All.—

 Freezin' an' fiercely, fiercely an' freezin',

 The wintry-laden breezes blaw ;

 But what care we for wind or snaw,

 Aroun' the ingle bleezin' ! *

---

* See Appendix.

EPISTLE TO JOHN MARR.

*Composed after reading " Tibbie Shiel's in Yarrow " and
an encouraging letter on some of my verses : Poem
and criticism both from the pen of Prof. John Stuart
Blackie.*

DEAR MARR :—Your letter cam' yestreen,
  And wow ! it made me canty ;
The Great Tribune to be my frien',
  Is honour far frae scanty.
And here ye see I've tried my han',
  In far aff Camden city
To imitate the Grand Old Man,
  And his inspiring ditty !

It's worthy o' the fruitful times,
  When Scott was in his glory ;

When Wordsworth trill'd the triple rhymes
   Renowned in song and story.
It has the happy, hearty ring,
   Few living bards can marrow;
Bravo, old poet, thus to sing,
   Of Tibbie Shiel's in Yarrow!

But faith nae ferlie tho' he soar,
   Aboon his generation;
Sma' wonder we're enraptur'd o'er,
   This sang o' his creation!
Wha's sipp'd like him frae sic a brew,
   And quaff'd wi' sic a quorum
The undiluted mountain-dew
   Dispensed in Tibbie's jorum?

O, hoo my Muse would sparkle forth,
   In panegyrics metric
If I had fish'd a day wi' North,
   Or Hogg, the bard o' Ettrick!

Or coost a line by Stoddart's side,

Or trod the foot-path narrow

Wi' Blackie in his prime and pride,

Upon the banks of Yarrow!

In guid braid Scots I would have built,

My rhythmic lines together,

The language o' the plaid and kilt,

The thistle and the heather.

In Scotch the Yarrow first was sung,

And nane will tarry langer

Than that rare ballad in the tongue

Of Hamilton o' Bangour!

For sweet melodious rippling verse,

Romantic or historic ;

Nae Cockney singers to asperse,

I'll choose the darling Doric !

While Sass'nach sangs are hard and harsh,

As screetchy as a barrow,

And muddy as an English marsh,
  The Scotch resemble Yarrow!

Alas, that I the truth should own,
  Thus far on life's short journey,
Tho' years a score in Caledon
  I never saw the burnie!
Confined at hame to ae puir spot
  Till Fortune seaward bore me,
The classic lands of Burns and Scott
  Are unexplored before me!

This prosy land provides for me
  Nae sheep nor tunefu' shepherd,
The salmon I'm aloo'd to see
  Are either cann'd or kipper'd!
And what o'er a' the lave is mair
  A poet's soul to harrow,
My Tweed's the drumlie Delaware,
  A slimy ditch my Yarrow!

Nae hill rears high its heath-clad crest,

But sand heaps in abundance

Shed burrs on Nature's brawny breast

In unco great redundance.

Instead o' roun' a lake to tramp

Wi' rifle and retriever,

I hugger owre a dismal swamp

And fecht the chills and fever !

Nae lark regales me in the morn

Wi' bursts o' sang spasmodic ;

The strain that on the breeze is borne

At nicht comes frae the puddick !

Throughout the day I'm glad to hear

The chirpin' o' a sparrow,

And dream about the birds that cheer

The dowie dens o' Yarrow !

And whyles when I wi' leisure blest

Set oot to tak' a daunder,

Gang North or Sooth, or East or West,

    Whaurever I may wander,

Nae bonny lass wi' glances sweet

    Repays me for my roamin',

The maist it is my luck to meet

    Are dusky as the gloamin'!

    In spite of a' I sing my sang,

        And tho' I'm aften weary,

    The better day to come or lang

        Aye keeps my courage cheery!

    I look for mony a merry rant

        Ere Death let's fling his arrow,

    And not the least will be my jaunt

        To see the Braes o' Yarrow!

Feb. 21, 1892.

SONNET—HARRY GAULD.

(In the lingo o' the "Lum'.")

A KEEN aul' man : I min' 'im fairly weel ;

I see 'im yet wi' glitt'rin', glancin' pow,

His fat roun' face as reid's the fiery lowe,

As back an fore he dairtit in 'is skweel !

Fin eence aroos'd his rage wiz ill to queel,

An' tho' his tongue wiz fit aneuch ti' cowe

The loodest racket or the biggest row,

He swung 'his strap wi' mair than or'nar' skeel !

Twa scenes come back, abeen the rest, ti' me :

A wintry morn I saw 'im at the Stroop,

Richt blythe an' early for 'is daily scrub ;

An' that daft day his scholars in their glee,

Poot sklates an' skawlies in 'is pot o' soup,

An' pitcht 'is pet cat "Tigger" i' the dub !

TO A. L. LAW, RICHMOND HILL, L.I.

*On receiving copy of " A Visit to the Tap o' Noth," by W
Stephen, November 4th, 1887.*

DEAR LAW :—Wi' interest I hae read
    The screed o' Rhymer Stephen ;
And tho' in fairness be it said,
    The lines are gey uneven.
Tho' somewhat caulrif' is the sang,
    A critic maun remember,
The road was rough he had to gang,
    The month was bleak November !
So for a first attempt it's fair,
    And readers rais'd near Rhynie ;
Will con it o'er wi' pleasure rare,
    When far across the briny.

It mentions names o' auld langsyne,

 Alas ! noo gettin' fogy ;

And brings a hunner mair to min'

 Alang the vale o' Bogie.

Rough as the verses are and rude,

 They hae the necromancy

To start in one the musing mood,

 And touch the springs o' fancy.

So thanks for sending me the strain,

 Composed by rhymer Stephen ;

I've answer'd it in hamely vein,

 And aince again we're even !

March 4, 1892.

IN MEMORIAM: WILLIAM MACLENNAN.

Champion Dancer and Bagpipe player. Died at
Montreal, Oct. 30, 1892.

THRO' Canada's forests the chill winds were sighin',
    Despoilin' the trees o' their verdure sae braw,
And 'a' that was bonny in Nature was dyin',
    When Willie was also by Death ta'en awa' !

O, whaur is the Dancer could trip it so neatly,
    And whaur is the piper that ever could blaw
So stirrin' a blast, yet so saftly and sweetly,
    As Willie, rare Willie that noo is awa' !

Lang, lang will it be or his laurels shall wither,
    And Highlands and Lowlands for lang we may ca'

Afore Caledonia can gie's sic anither
  To add to her glory like him that's awa' !

Harsh Fortune ! we canna haud back frae complainin',
  When bosoms are burstin' the tears they maun fa' !
And talented, modest, blythe-hearted MacLennan
  We'll never forget him tho' noo he's awa'.

TO WM. M. CALLINGHAM,

On being Recommended to Write in English.

DEAR CALLINGHAM :—I shall give heed to your com-
ment concise—to practise English is indeed the soundest
of advice. None knows it better than the bard, this
precept that you preach ; but ah ! it pains and grieves
me hard to slight my native speech. To change out-
right my Scottish rhyme for yours I would be loth ; I
cherish hopes in course of time to make my mark in
both. Unconquer'd as the Celts of old remains the
tongue I prize, and yet, tho' none more brave and bold,
not slow to compromise. So, if you please, as Scotland's
King annex'd the English throne, I'll try to sound an
English string in union with mine own. Not by com-
pulsion, but by choice—to take or to refuse—(let friends
bewail or foes rejoice !)—if sanctioned by the Muse.
And when I tempt my doubtful fate, before you look for
blots, dear boy you must reciprocate and sing a song in
Scots !

TO ALEXANDER NICOLL.

On Returning Some Books.

KIND SIR :—Wi' thanks baith big an' mony
I send ye hame your bookies bonny,
And if they hae been blauded ony
      In my possession,
Weel pleased I'll pay the fine, dear crony,
      For my transgression.

Tho' lately press'd for leisure sair
(And books like thae need muckle care !)
I managed ilka day to spare
      An 'oor or twa,
To pang my noddle wi' their lear',
      And man it's braw !

O, ane an' a' they pleased me weel,

But, sir, my choice I'll nae conceal,

The poets showed sic happy skeel,

   Sic rowth o' rhymes,

I kissed their pages in my zeal

    A score o' times !

For this my gratitude is due—

And do you doubt my he'rt is fu' ?—

I pray wi' a' my soul for you,

   Whae'er may miss them,

That ye'll get books, baith auld and new,

    Whene'er ye wiss them !

May Time ne'er land ye in a pickle ;

May tears o' grief ne'er frae ye trickle ;

Lang may it be till Death's fell sickle

   Shall mak' ye fa',

And lang I hope I'll coont on Nicoll

    As frien' to Law !

June 25, 1883.

SONG—THE WOODS O' CLOVA.

THE Bonny Woods o' Clova
How can I e'er forget?
I've wander'd far but never seen
The equal o' them yet.
Frae sunny brae to shady glen
An' burnie singin' doon the den—
O, ilka nook I used to ken
Within the Woods o' Clova!

The Bonny Woods o' Clova
Look doon aboon my hame,
Wee village wi' a charm for me
Nae ither spot can claim.

On ilka side the hills arise

Whaur Nature dons her fairest guise,

And half-way tow'ring to the skies

    Are seen the Woods o' Clova !

The Bonny Woods o' Clova !

    The langer I'm awa'

Aye dearer still, if that could be,

    I lo'e them ane an' a'.

'Twas there my musings were begun,

There first my rustic rhymes were spun,

And my dear lass was woo'd an' won

    Amang the Woods o' Clova !

The Bonny Woods o' Clova !

    At times my he'rt grows sair

When thochts come in my heid that I

    May never view them mair.

But surely Fate will be sae kin'
As bear me back across the brine
To meet the frien's o' auld lang syne
    An' see the Woods o' Clova !

The Bonny Woods o' Clova,
    Forever may they bide
The brawest sicht to gaze upon
    In a' the country side !
Had I the future in my han'
For happier days I'd never plan
Than end my life whaur it began—
    Beside the Woods o' Clova !

A FAMILIAR EPISTLE TO THE HON. WM. BURNS SMITH, CHICAGO, ILLS.

DEAR SMITH,—Gin it was in my micht
Thro' airy realms to tak' a flicht,
I'd seek Chicago oot the nicht,*
    And single-handed
Would never seek to lag or licht
    Till there I landed.

But, sir, that I should hae to sing,
We're nae at fleein' worth a thing ;
The meanest bird that flaps a wing
    Can beat us hollow,
And when it mak's its shortest spring
    We daurna follow !

---

* Oration by Ingersoll on Burns at the Chicago Auditorium.

Still, Thought, dear friend, is unconfined,

Nae Space impedes the March o' Mind,

So here at hame I sit resigned,

  And think I see ye,

But wishin' Fate had been as kind

  As placed me wi' ye !

For, faith, I dootna but the noo

Rare Ingersoll has made his boo

And startit in to tell ye hoo

  Oor darlin' Robbie

Ootrivall'd a' the rhymin' crew

  At their ain hobby !

I'd coont it like a gowden dream

To list to ocht from one I deem

In Eloquence and Wit supreme,

  For nane come near him ;

And sic a man on sic a theme,—

  O, but to hear him !

In mony a polish'd prosy phrase
We've tributes penn'd in Bobby's praise ;
And since the gloamin' o' his days
To heeze his glory
Oor bards hae trampit ithers' taes
To sing his story !

But this you're hearin' as I write *
(Wi' purple ink on paper white !)
Frae Ingersoll, the godless wight,
In points that bristle,
Will knock past records "out of sight"
As clean's a whistle !

Of a' men livin' he's the man
That best I think can understan'
The Beauty and the Wisdom gran',
The pride, the passion,

---

* The whole epistle entirely extemporaneous.

That glint frae Burns on ilka han'
    Like di'monds flashin'!

Nay, was not Scotia's darling Bard
An Ingersollian in regard
To Kirks and Creeds he lash'd sae hard
        In prose and metre?
Oor later Bob has never daur'd
        To *saut* them *sweeter!*

Wi' great impatience I shall bide
The passin' o' the time and tide
And trains that cross the distance wide
        'Twixt you and Camden,
Till doon my throat baith hair and hide *
        The Speech I've cramm'd in!

---

* "And horns," I might also add, expecting it to be a deil of a production of course!

Till then—that is until I see

The printed page afore my e'e,

This letter, crony, tak' frae me

    In frien'ly token :

We'll die content since Robert G.

    On Burns has spoken !

January 23, 1893.

SONG—JAMIE NICOLL.

WITHIN a bonny Hielan' strath
  Far frae the sicht or soun' of ocean,
Whaur trains hae never made a path
  Nor traction-engines raised commotion,
There sits a cosy fairm we'll say
  That neither little is nor mickle,
Whaur lives the hero o' my lay,
  A splendid chiel ca'd Jamie Nicoll.

Chorus :—

Honest Jamie, canny Jamie,
  Canty, cheery Jamie Nicoll,
Of a' the men I chance to ken
  Commen' me aye to Jamie Nicoll !

He is a horseman ticht an' trig
    An' weel can guide the ploo or harrow,
And while upon the lang hairst rig
    The pairish canna boast his marrow.
In ony branch he'll stan' a han'
    Frae trailin' rake to wieldin' sickle,
Altho' I say't there's few that can,
    Keep up a day wi' Jamie Nicoll !

Chorus.

The gift o' singin' sangs is his,
    And wha can tell a story better ?
His comic style and funny phiz,
    Would please the maist forjaskit crater.
He is a chap would gar ye lauch,
    Till owre your nose the tears would trickle ;
O, dinna brag o' Mansie Wauch,
    Till ye hae met wi' Jamie Nicoll !

Chorus.

13

Hoo he can please his fellow-man,

    Is aye to him his foremost study ;

And ever ready is his han'

    To help a poor and honest body.

Tho' doun on shams and a' pretence,

    He ne'er would leave ye in a pickle ;

O, for a Scot in ilka sense,

    Commen' me aye to Jamie Nicoll !

    Honest Jamie, cannie Jamie,

        Canty, cheery Jamie Nicoll ;

    Of a' the men I chance to ken,

        Commen' me aye to Jamie Nicoll.

PER PHONOGRAPH.

To Frien's in Auld Scotia. Recorded at Philadelphia, December 16th, 1892. Phonogram in Aberdeen at present writing.

SOME gie their news on postal-cairds,
    Some write a great lang letter;
And some for sendin' brief regairds,
    Think telegrams are better.
But this invention dings them a',
    Whaure'er ye may gang seekin';
For noo without a crack or flaw,
    Ye hear me plainly speakin'.
I'm nae great han', as ye can tell,
    At makin' an oration;
But what ye get is frae mysel',
    My very ain dictation.
Jist cock your lugs an' watch my mou',
    It fairly cowes the gowan;

Tho' ragin' seas between us noo
  Three thoosan' miles are rowin'.
Ev'n Death, my tongue it canna stay,
  Nae maitter what befa' me ;
Ye still can hear me say my say,
  As weel as gin ye saw me !

Gin we could only but gang back,
  And catch frae lang deid sages
Some samples o' the wye they spak',
  In their respective ages.
Could we but listen to a bard
  Like Shakespeare, at oor pleasure ;
Or Burns, lang laid below the sward,
  O, what a priceless treasure !
The worth o' books we'll ne'er forget,
  Nor in oor praise be stintin' ;
But Human Speech is greater yet
  Than writin' or than printin'.

Time's up ! so I maun say Good-bye,
 Tho' laith I am to leave ye ;
But better stop wi' grace, say I,
 Than simply gab to deave ye.
Guid luck I wish ye frae my he'rt,
 Whae'er ye are that hearken ;
May sorrow never be your pairt,
 Nor want your dwellin' darken.
As my auld Uncle used to say,
 Gin we will only DEE weel ;
Eenoo, forever and for aye,
 The chances are we'll BE weel.

"GO AND SIN NO MORE."

Ae Sunday in Jerusalem,
   The crafty Scribes and Pharisees,
While Christ preached in the kirk to them,
   Brocht him (unless the Bible lees),
A single woman they had fan'
Carousin' wi' a mairriet man,
And that there could be nae mistak',
Had captured in the very ack.

" See here's," said they, "a sinfu' jaud,
   And here's a bag that's fu' o' stanes ;
Gin we should dee as Moses bade,
   We'd gar them crack against her banes.
Come, Jesus, noo ; ye ken the law,
Should this coorse quine be loot awa' ?

Nae backin' doon, the question's clear,

What should we do, gin we may speir ? "

They thocht to trip Him wi' the case,

   And some to jeer Him had begun ;

When frae the mob He turned His face,

   And stoopin' doonwards to the grun',

His fingers usin' for a pen,

He wrote what nane could comprehen',

Oblivious to the murmurs lood,

That issued frae the tauntin' crood.

But roos'd by their ootcries at last

   He lookit straucht to whaur they war,

And as their een on Him they cast

   Says He " Since ye sae anxious are,

To ken what is the thing to dee,

This answer kindly tak' frae Me :

Whaever o' ye has nae sin

To hit the lassie may begin ! "

And syne again He bent Him doon
  To write upon the grun' some mair,
And a' the men that thranged aroun'
  Were self-convicted then and there :
The auldest cheil first turned aboot
An' like a thief he sneakit oot,
Yea, ane by ane, sae did they a'
Doon to the youngest slink awa'.

When Jesus lookit up again,
  According as the Scriptures tell,
Lo, there the woman stood her lane,
  Or nae ane wi' her but Himsel' ;
Syne says He to the dame, " My dear,
" Whaur are the fowk that brocht ye here ?
Did nae ane o' them raise a han' ? "
" Nay, sir," she answer'd, " Not a man."

Then answer'd Jesus, " Nor will I,
  Condemn ye tho' ye hae done wrang,

Stop ye your greetin', tak' your wye,

   But dee the richt as on ye gang "—

A kindly, short reproof that may

Hae touch'd her mair I'm bold to say,

And wrocht in her a better cure

Than tho' He'd lectured her an hoor !

REFLECTIONS ON THE WA'-GOIN' O' EIGHTY-TWA.

AULD year, I fear for you at last,
The hinmost die has noo been cast ;
Your son comes postin' thro' the blast,
   And Eichty-twa,
You'll soon be number'd wi' the past,
    You're near awa' !

Lang hae ye dwelt amang us here,
Your very name to us is dear ;
Ah ! weel do you deserve a tear
   Oor grief to shaw,
But you'll be thocht on, never fear,
    When you're awa' !

Sin' first ye socht to show your face,

What change ye've wrocht amang oor race ;

Ev'n kings and queens to you may trace

    Their rise or fa',

And you'll be mourned in ilka place

    When you're awa' !

We fouth o' frien's hae tint by thee,

Some stown by Death—some owre the sea,

And ithers lost on little plea,

    Or cause ava,

On this or that we fail'd to gree,

    And they're awa' !

In thee we've found some new anes too,

And some hae aye stood firm and true,

Nae maitter what cauld bliffarts blew,

    Aroun' oor ha',

They lent a hand to help us thro'

    Nor gaed awa' !

Hoo aft within your fickle reign

Oor wyes we hae resolved to men',

And yet hoo aft and aft agen

             Broke voos and a'—

We couldna tell ye aince in ten,

             But that's awa' !

Some craters thocht ye pinched them sair,

And kept their boards and bodies bare,

And nocht again did ithers care,

             Wi' pension braw,

They hadna far to scrape whene'er

             It gaed awa' !

For me—it's jist as gospel true—

My little purse has twice been fu',

Sin' first ye burst upon my view

             Half smor'd in snaw ;

But poun's an' pennies lang or noo

             Hae flown awa' !

Fareweel auld frien', it's plain to me

That ye hae plumed your wings to flee,

And soon oot owre baith land and sea

> While tempests blaw,

Auld Time will ken by Auchty-three

> That you're awa'!

OOR AIN WEE HAME.

"To mak' a happy fireside clime
To weans and wife,
That's the true pathos and sublime
Of human life!"

THE wind comes moanin' o'er the ice-bound river,
The caul'rif cloods are scuddin' to the sea,
Wee birdies roun' the windows coo'er and shiver
Withoot the shelter o' a leafy tree.

The frost this mornin' made its mark at zero,
Soon aifter denner cam' a rainy thaw,
And in the evenin' it wad ta'en a hero
To made a journey thro' the slush and snaw.

But supper's past, an' seated in my "study,"
  My slippers toastin' at the cheerfu' fire,
I've nae remembrance o' the roadways muddy,
  Wi' a' aroun' me to my heart's desire.

Duff's in a corner wi' his slate and scawlie,
  And Nanette's tyauvin' wi' her doll and broom ;
They're man and mistress, and they're doin' brawlie
  At keepin' hoosie in their papa's room.

Up frae the kitchen comes a flood o' singin',
  It's mamma liltin' to the waukrif' wean,
And as her ballads to the roof come ringin',
  I'm fain to listen and to rest my een.

But Time's so precious that I daurna dally
  To cheer my journey wi' my helpmate's sang,
For soon 'twould waft me to the happy valley,
  Whaur I micht loiter by the way owre lang.

O, cruel Fate! that leaves so poor a portion
  Of precious time that I may coont my ain!
O, sordid Age! as stoop to sic extortion
  To stint the product o' my he'rt and brain!

My Guardian Spirit, gin it be your pleasure,
  I'll nae petition ye for gowd nor gear,
But grant, I beg of you, a little leisure,
  And thanks I'll waft ye wi' a he'rt sincere!

If 'tis your will to keep my table scanty,
  My claes in tatters, and my fireside cauld,
Gin left wi' leisure I can still be canty,
  And at my lot shall neither sulk nor scauld.

As things are noo I'll own I'm discontented,
  Some days nae muckle, but the neist some mair,
And truth to tell I would gang clean demented
  If Hope should knuckle to the fiend Despair.

I gulp my brak'fast, an' begin my yokin'
    The hinmost quarter past the chap o' sax,
An' twal' hoors later at my hame I'm knockin',
    Gin thro' the day I've met wi' nae mistak's.

But as a recompense for a' my drudgin',
    (There's nae plant livin' but some sunshine keps !),
Life's tribulations doon the road gang trudgin'
    The very minute that I mount the steps.

Then, like a torrent, comes the merry clatter
    Of childish voices thro' the bolted door,
And troubles scatter at the pitter-patter
    Of Duff and Nanette as they cross the floor.

" Is that you, papa ? "—and, as " yes " I answer,
    My boy receives me with a happy face,
And Nancy, jumpin' like a merry-dancer,
    Obstructs my passage with a fond embrace.

14

Ben to the kitchen I am then escorted,
  Where mamma ready has the table spread,
And Baby Stella, in her chair supported,
  Loups up to greet me as she hears my tread.

Twa chubby hands rax oot to grab my glaisses,
  And, as a ransom for their safe release,
A score o' kisses and o' fond caresses
  Are shower'd upon her or I think to cease.

Then mamma, lookin' aye so bricht an' cheery,
  Brings on the supper and pours oot the tea,
And frae that minute I forget I'm weary,
  And wish a' creatures were as blest as we!

Syne come the letters and the evening papers,
  The social chat, in which the youngest shares,
The laddie's lessons and the lassic's capers,
  And a' the tellin' o' the day's affairs.

Hoo mamma started to the weekly washin',

    That had been steepin' in the tubs for days,

When rain in pailfu's frae the lift cam' plashin',

    And put a damper on her hopes—and claes.

Hoo hens that were sae thrawn for a' the sizzen,

    As nae to bless us wi' the sicht o' eggs,

Had since the mornin' gi'en us half a dizzen,

    Sae big an' bonny as to fairly fleg's.

Hoo Duff was gettin' that he liked his schoolin',

    And had done splendid in the bypast week ;

Hoo Nanette teased him wi' her constant foolin',

    Hoo little Stella had begun to speak !

Or I may treat them to a hamespun story

    O' some adventure in the steerin' toun,

Whaur some for fortune (and a few for glory !)

    Wear oot existence in the daily roun'.

And syne when mamma starts to wash the dishes,
  To please the baby I may play buffoon,
Or like a soldier (as the darling wishes),
  Gang marchin' wi' her while I sowff a tune.

So when the clock upon the shelf starts ringin',
  A warnin' to me to gang up the stair,
I only manage to escape by bringin'
  Some trick or wile upon the bairns to bear.

Then Duff comes sneakin' in a trice ahin' me,
  By Nanette follow'd in sae saft a style,
That in the tactics they adopt to win me
  To let them enter, I am forced to smile.

Wi' sic a twasome I could never quarrel,
  And while I dootless micht do mair in peace,
I wadna for the poet's fairest laurel
  Desire the clatter that they mak' to cease.

I like to listen to their guileless prattle,
  Where youth and quaintness are so sweetly blent,
So roun' aboot me they can run and rattle,
  And chirp and chatter to their hearts' content.

But a'thing sometime maun come till an endin',
  And soon I see them, by their mamma led,
Like pictured angels, thro' the doorway wendin',
  In snawy nichtgoons, to their cosy bed.

I follow aifter to assist to hap them,
  To get their blessin' and their sweet " Good-nicht!"
And fondly wish them, as I kiss and clap them,
  A blythe awaukenin' wi' the mornin's licht.

Then mamma joins me wi' her sewin' maybe,
  (For ever eident maun the poor folk plod!)
Or tries again to get the sleepless baby,
  By singin', wafted to the Land o' Nod.

I sit an' muse, an' mak' a feint to scribble,
　But ilka sentence, whether prose or rhyme,
Comes frae my pen wi' sic a weary dribble,
　The poor results are hardly worth the time.

I start to dream, and in my dreams am airted
　To moors and meadows hyne across the sea,
And wander thro' them just as lichtsome-he'rted,
　As when a laddie 'twas my wont to be.

Again I live amang my bygane pleasures,
　By fancy wafted far beyond the deep,
But when I try to realise my treasures,
　I start to find that I hae been asleep:

To find the paradise I almost tasted
　Like mist has vanished as I raise my head,
And naething's left me but an evening wasted,
　And Conscience hintin' that it's time for bed!

Oor Ain Wee Hame.

For noo, wide-wauken'd, I maun seek my chaumer,
    And very rarely do I steek a styme
Till clocks and ferry-bells wi' dinsome clamor
    Hae waked the echoes wi' the midnicht chime.

Thus runs the record at the present writin';
    As this day's story so my ithers are,
And tho' to some it may look uninvitin',
    There is a life that I could relish waur.

Tho' some ahead o' us in Wealth hae sprinted,
    And some thro' Fortune hae been set mair high,
We've Youth and Health and Happiness unstinted,
    A triple blessing that nae gowd can buy!

                .   .   .   .
                .   .   .   .

January, 1893.

A FLYING TRIP.

An extempore rhyme delivered at the Complimentary Supper tendered
to Mr. GEORGE C. WATSON, on his return from Scotland, August
6th, 1890, by the Philadelphia Camerons.

THE month o' June was wearin' doon, the torrid
days were comin',

Big folk had a' vacation bees within their bonnets
bummin,'

When ane we ken, but needna name within oor tale
romantic,

Packed up his duds, and steer'd for hame, across the
wild Atlantic !

O, my ! the bonny sichts he saw, wi' seas atween us
'rowin',

Within the compass o' a month !—It fairly cowes the
gowan !

The pictures that he glow'red upon !—Columbus nor De Gama
Would ever dreamt or daured to dream o' sic a panorama !

There first we see him on the sea, frae daylicht doun to gloaming,
Paradin' wi' impatient stride the swift an' sure "Wyoming ; "
And hardly had she touched her slip when, like a meteor shootin'
He left the Captain and the crew wi' Cockney lads disputin',
An tore a swath thro' nicht an' day,—thro' Englan' an' thro' Scotlan',
At sic a pace as micht gar Time forevermair gang dottlin' ;
Nor did he slack for aince his speed, the hero o' my ditty,
Until the smell o' Finnan fish proclaimed the Granite City !

Syne aff he jumps an' shak's the han' o' mony a weel
    lo'ed cronie,
Than Bon-Accordians' warmer he'rts are nae in
    Caledonie !

    But Steam alas ! it winna stay, an' George he daurna
        dacker ;—
A train's like luck, gin aince she's tint ye'll nevermair
    o'ertak her !
A score o' miles maun yet be cross'd, and he can nae be
    stannin',
And so he gangs and books a berth that brings him to
    LUMPHANAN !
But e'en at hame he canna rest, impelled by some mad
    speerit,
He prances here an' dances there as if gane clean
    deleerit !
Nae scene is passed, nae haunt is missed amang his ex-
    plorations,—
Deeside aince mair becomes his ain wi' a' its thirty
    stations !

The day he pokes aboot at hame an' wakes the
    chords o' pathos !

The morn gangs doun and prees the pig at Mill o' Hirn
    in Crathes !

An' neist perchance, tak's in Rob Roy, that guards the
    road to Culter ;

An' spen's the evenin' crackin' jokes wi' Tailor and wi'
    Souter !

Anon gangs up to Lochnagar that's famed for Crags and
    Whiskey,

And tests a sample o' the stuff that keeps it's frien's sae
    frisky !

And wha's to ken the Queen hersel' perchance the lad
    may corral,

An' drag him doun to spend the day aroond aboot
    Balmoral !

Then neist in coach and four he'll join Carnegie, King
    o' Cluny,

And wake the echoes o' the hills wi'—" Little Annie
    Rooney ! "

O, wha can tell the pranks he play'd amang the
dears and dawties,
That paint their cheeks wi' porridge pots and peel and
eat pitawties !
I'll bet my head that mony a tear frae mony an e'e cam'
startin'
When Geordie strapp'd his trunks aince mair, an' spak
to them o' partin' !

Again we turn the glass to find oor spry and sportive
rover
Conversin' wi' McGinty's ghost within the straits o'
Dover !
The banks o' Dee then gay *Pareé*, that held the Ex-
position,
And Eiffel's awful Iron Tooer that dings a' crockanition !
Syne back again the wye he gaed, that naething may be
undone
He spens his hinmost hoors amang the sichts and soun's
o' London !

He scours the toun frae East to West, and nae afraid to
grapple

E'en Jack the Ripper in his den, gangs peerin' thro'
Whitechapel !

Draps in to see the Grand Old Man ajist afore he leave
land,

And gies him points on Jamie Blaine's next fecht wi'
Grover Cleveland !

George Francis Train and Nellie Bly !—New York
and you, Tacoma !

Roun' whilk there hovered for a while a whiff o' Fame's
aroma,

Gae, steek your gabs and hide your heids for ever and
for ever !

Your flichts may sair the Stars an' Stripes, but Caledonians—Never !

We grant ye quick at antrin jaunts, but for a record
breaker

Commen' me to that wale o' men,—A canny Scoto-
Quaker !

Then here we've come to drink his health, that stopt for
    aye their yaumerins,
Thrice worthy o' his high degree,—Past Chieftain o' the
    Camerons!
Since last we met he's braved life's ills frae billows doun
    to barnacles,
An' may he aye as happy be as here the nicht at
    Hornickels!

ST. ROBERT'S NICHT IN ALBANY.*

(Read at 40th Anniversary Banquet of Albany Burns Club, January 25, 1893.)

LANGSYNE—an' maybe nae sae lang,

Burns birthday aye brocht oot a thrang

O' fallows that wi' Speech an' Sang

 Had happy Nichts in Albany !

At sican splores it was a treat

To see rare Dickson † on his feet,

Or hae a lilt frae Alfred Street ‡

 The famous bard o' Albany.

---

* By special request.

† James Dickson, Esq., first President of the Club.

‡ The poet Alfred B. Street, former member of the Club.

Since then near thirty years hae sped

Across oor auld Dutch City's head,

And ither folks are here instead

　　To honor Burns in Albany !

While yet the Nicht is in its prime

We'll call the roll in rippling rhyme

That cronies o' a future time

　　May ken wha were in Albany !

There's first an' foremost famous Neil,*

A clever, jolly, Paisley chiel,

As president he answers weel,

　　A credit aye to Albany !

There's Jamie Milne † frae Binghamtoun,

A great lang-heidit, learn-ed loon,

---

* Hon. Neil Gilmour, late State Superintendent of Public Instruction, President of Club.

† Dr. James M. Milne, now President Oneouta Normal School.

And so the Nicht we've set him doon

    To speak on "Burns" in Albany!

There's next a Yankee legal licht,*

Wi' pow and een aye bleezin' bricht,

He's gaun to sing a sang the nicht

    To please the folks in Albany!

Then comes a double-barrel'd Scott, †

Crammed to the mou' wi' Gospel shot,

"Scotch Literature" 's the text he's got

    To preach upon in Albany!

Our Mayor ‡ next, tho' young, nae weak,

On "Oor adopted Toun" will speak,

And doobtless he could raise a reek

    And tell the truth on Albany!

---

* Frederick Hadhams, Esq., of Albany.

† Rev. W. Q. Scott, of 1st Presbyterian Church.

‡ Hon. James H. Manning, Mayor of Albany.

Then into sang again we'll slide

And hear a callant * chant wi' pride

The pleasures o' oor " Ain Fireside,"

As they're enjoy'd in Albany !

Syne will we hae oor frien' Kinnear †

A' bubblin' ower wi' ancient lear'

To tell us hoo we cam' to heir

The Monument in Albany !

And then we'll get in splendid style ‡

A twa three minutes to beguile

" There was a lad was born in Kyle "—

Whose Statue stands in Albany !

---

* Mr. Wm. D. MacFarlane, of Albany.

† Peter Kinnear, Esq., President of Southend Bank, to whom Albany is indebted for the magnificent Burns' monument in Washington Park.

‡ By Mr. Thomas Impett, of Troy.

Noo, lo ! upon the list there comes

The pick o' Pedagogic chums*

Hyne a' the wye frae Barrie's " Thrums "

To speak a bit in Albany !

Then next oor luck has till us row'd

A chiel that's worth his wecht in gowd,

Scotch-Irish Dr. James Macleod, †

The Rev'rend Wit of Albany !

And would the cronies like to know

The debt to Walter Scott we owe,

It will be tauld by " flowery Joe," ‡

The Ingersoll o' Albany !

Judge Woods § will then be given the floor

To speak a word for Thomas Moore,

---

* Wm. J. Milne, LL.D., President of State Normal College.

† Rev. James M'Leod, D.D., of 1st Congregational Church.

‡ Joseph A. Lawson, Editor, *Fort Orange Monthly.*

§ Hon. F. H. Woods, Surrogate of Albany Co.

Yet fond o' " Robbie " at the core

As ony Scot in Albany !

Buchanan * next will charm us a',

As fine a chiel as e'er ye saw ;

Expert at War as skilled in Law,

And settled doon in Albany !

Then Montignani † will arise ;

His name Italian blood implies,

But he's for a' the thick disguise

As true a Scot's in Albany !

O mony mair frae far an' near

In Robbie's name are gather'd here,

And may we meet for mony a year

To honor Burns in Albany !

---

* Major Charles J. Buchanan, of Albany.
† John F. Montignani, Esq., of Albany, Secretary of the Club.

Oor Statue stan's o'er a' the rest,

And time to come will yet attest

O' Clubs to Robert Burns the best

    And greatest will be Albany !

Then royal honors to his name,

The poet o' the he'rt and hame,

Wi' jealous care we'll guard his fame

    While lives a Scot in Albany !

January, 1893.

THE THRIFTY THREE.

For a number of years it was the custom of THE NORTH AMERICAN
UNITED CALEDONIAN ASSOCIATION to give a prize for the
best essay submitted at their annual meeting. In 1888 the
Secretary of the Organization made a new departure with the
results as faithfully chronicled in the following effusion.

" Thrift, thrift, Horatio ! "

SAID Smith with neither brag nor bluff :

" Of Essays and such prosy stuff

Langsyne we've surely had enough,

    For once we'll change our key ;

Let's show our Rhymers (few reward),

Their verse we hold in high regard,

Here's Burns (by Gebbie) for the bard

    That sends the best to me ! "

In Canada for Scotchmen famed

The Clansmen met and soon proclaimed

Three canny critics had been named

    To judge the sonnets slee ;

But oh ! they were a *petty* lot,

Altho' a *glosso-graphic* Scot,

And *clerkie,* quick to spy a blot

    Were in the Thrifty Three !

Straucht to the settlin' were they set

Before their whistles had been wet,

Sma' ferlie then they should forget

    The task they had to dee ;

Sma' wonder sniffs o' mountain-dew

And glints o' gill-stoups sparklin' fu'

Should obfuscate the mental view

    Of Willie's Thrifty Three !

And thus decreed they, ane and a',

The lilts were nae the thing ava,

'Twould be but siller thrown awa
    A gift sic stuff to gie,—
Nae ane o' a' the stanzas sent
Were worth the permanence o' print !—
And " Deil a dollar shall be spent ! ! !"—
    (Signed) " Scotia's Thrifty Three."

O Time tak's maist unthocht o' turns,
Oor promised joys she aft adjourns ;
And bides wi' Gebbie still-a Burns
    He thocht for sure to see
Converted into gowd anon,—
But then he hadna coontit on
Encountrin' sic a Rubicon
    As formed the Thrifty Three !

And wise and witty Willie Smith,
For a' your pooer and a' your pith
They've made your " PRIZE " a muckle myth,
    Your offer look a lee ;

But never mind !—they hained your wealth !

Let Rancour rave and fling its filth,

'Twill cost you less to drink their health,—

Immortal Thrifty Three ! *

---

* This was published anonymously on hearing of the IN-decision, and soon afterwards the Author (a Competitor) was awarded the Prize.

FROM EPISTLE TO JOHN M'INTOSH,
A BROTHER BARD.

. . . .

Wi' you I'm in my glory, Johnnie,
And wadna change my place wi' ony ;
The words come slidin' aye sae bonny
   Frae oot your mou',
I wadna wish a better crony
   Than ane like you.

. . . .

Oor Life is like a stiff campaign :
Some sunny blinks wi' lots o' rain :
We aften strive for little gain
   When a's been done;
But still they dinna fecht in vain
   That stan' their grun' !

. . . .

While we hae got the pooer an' chance

We needna sit when we can dance;

We shouldna stan' when to advance

      Would be a gain;

Nor yet for aye on Circumstance

      Should we complain !

Anither thing we'll nae lose he'rt

Cause some can ca' a bonnier cairt,

And wi' mair flourish can assert

      Their schemes to man,

But try to act our humble pairt

      The best we can.

Tho' lilies bloom wi' charms replete,

And roses wi' the dew-draps weet

O'er a' oor tended flooers are sweet,

      That's nae a plea

Why gowans sma' amang oor feet

      Should pine and dee.

Tho' lav'rocks lilt in heavenly key,

And throstles flood the woods wi' glee ;

Tho' mony birds may farrer flee

      And sweeter sing,

That's nae excuse for wrannies wee

        Their heads to hing !

So, sir, tho' some wi' brighter light,

Wi' firmer grasp and greater might,

May better sangs and talēs indite

      Than we can do,

That needna mak' us scared to write

        Nor shut oor mou'.

Some bashfu' bardie, wha's to ken,

In days to come may condescen'

To read oor chapter to the en',

      And frae the wark

Pluck courage up to try his pen

        And mak' his mark !

Then, Johnnie, lad, expand your chest,

We'll hae oor say as weel's the rest ;

And this I firmly would request,

        Tho' polyglots,

Because we ken its compass best

          We'll stick to Scots !

When wieldin' Reformation's rung ;

When citin' Saws for auld or young ;

When Sangs to touch the he'rt are sung,

        I tell ye true,

Oor couthie, hamely mither-tongue

          Will brawlie do !

June, 1883.

FROM EPISTLE TO JAMES SOUTAR.

WHEN Fancy wi' her maidens braw
Convoys me to her realm awa',
I sometimes rhyme a line or twa
      To please mysel',
Wi' nae intent my stuff to shaw,
      Nor ane to tell.

The SUMMER breezes, saft an' mild ;
The fields where AUTUMN sweet has smiled;
The gusty storms o' WINTER wild,
      The budding SPRING,—
They hae my heart so sair beguiled
      I hae to sing.

The gloamin' or the mornin' gray;

The hill-taps gilt wi' Phœbus' ray;

The burnie brattlin' doon the brae,

   And heavenwards hung,

The massy cloods, sae grand, sae gay

   Unlowse my tongue!

A bonnie flooerie wat wi' dew;

The lift wi' starnies blinkin' thro';

A birdie singin' sweet an' true

   On bush or tree;—

The poet looks: they live anew,

   Nae mair to dee!

A wooded, weird, romantic place,

Whaur witches run and warlocks race;

A sweet an' sonsy lassie's face,

   Whaur virtue beams,—

Ah, lad, I hinna far to chase,

   For rowth o' themes!

Some plainly say I should lat be
And nae provoke the critic's e'e,
For gin my work they were to see
   They'd ca' me " Coof!"
But feigh! that never troubles me,
  I'm critic-proof!

Whate'er I feel I'll try to say
Still in a manly hamely way;
Syne gin Reviewers choose to bray,
   Why then they can;
But for them I'll nae budge my tae
   Nor change my plan.

He wad be saft would stop his sang
For a' the castigatin' gang;
The bulk o' a' their lectures lang
   Are worthless trash;
Gin ae time richt they ten times wrang
  Apply the lash!

And maybe, man, for a' their lear',

When fled hae ninety years or mair,

As muckle fame my book may share

As their critique,

And so to hurkle in despair

I sanna seek !

May, 1883.

"MARY FAIR" SKETCHES.

The Village.

THE village noo is in a steer
    Frae ae en' to the ither,
For mony fowk frae far an' near
    Are gaither'd here thegither :
Wi' cairts an' gigs whaur they can stan
    O' ilka shape an' color,
The streets are lined on every han'
    An' never lookit fuller
        Than on this day.

The stables a' within the place
    Are filled to overflowin',

And parks and lanes and yards nae less

    Their cavalry are showin'.

The ostlers o' the inn wi' haste

    Frae horse to stable clatter,

And sairly they for time are press'd

    To keep the beasts in water

        And meat that day !

  .   .   .   .

    While yet the Fair is free o' fechts

    We'll wander o'er the Green.

The Market noo is at its hicht

    An' tricks experimented,

Forethocht comes soon aneuch wi' nicht

    And bawbees are na stinted.

Wi' din and dirdum every where

    To hear ane's hardly able

To. naething would it weel compare

    But jist a perfect Babel

        For soun' that day !

Aroun' the Stance are sweetie-stan's
   To sell the toys an' fairin',
Beside them bairns wi' itchin' han's
   An' greedy mou's are starin'.

.   .   .   .

Upon the brae a tinkler sits
   Amang his jugs an' pails,
Amusin' fowk 'twixt smokes an' spits,
   Wi' sangs an' funny tales.
And as he gets the tither groat,
   For fear his pouch micht spill
He stows it doon his thirsty throat
   In shape o' half a jill
         O' drink that day.

We noo come to the Whiskey tent
   Whaur rags and wags are jinkin',
And gie me but the money spent
   By young an' auld on drinkin'.

They pu' the ither shillin' oot
　And wi' their glasses clinkin',
Quaff ane anither's health aboot,
　Uncarin' and unthinkin'
　　　　　What's wared that day.

Here sits a Cabrach fairmer fu',
　His beard wi' slavers dreepin',
And tho' he's in the noisy crew
　As soun's a tap he's sleepin'.
Anon he starts upon his feet,
　And tries his tyke wi' swearin',
Then gie's him kisses aft and sweet
　Amid the laddies cheerin'
　　　　　Him weel that day !

There in the midst a couple stan'
　And by their lively jargon,
We ken they're tryin' a' they can,
　To bring aboot a bargain.

At last they've made it to their min',

And ere they've time to swither,

Wi' jill aboot the twa lads join

And drink to ane anither,

To seal't that day !

. . . .

EXTRACTS "FROM THE QUEEN'S FIDDLER."

(Speech after " The Battle o' Bon-Accord.")

Their glasses toom'd then cam' the cry
For me—mysel'—to mak' reply;
And so concurrin' hame-owre I—
As prood to air my platform-wits
  As ony would-be Knox,
That bangs the Bible into bits
  When barkin' frae his box,
On Nature's plan—richt aff o' han'
  Thus gabbit to the folks :

" Kind friens : Aboot the fecht we had

Lat's hear nae ither wird,

Deid lat it lie as did the lad

This nicht upon the yird.

O Frien's are few and far between,

Sic frien's at least as ye hae been ;

When I forget ye may I be—
Sent in a sieve to sail the sea ;
Oblivion hap me wi' its wing
Gin I turn oot a pick-thank thing !
It aye has been my fervent wiss
　　To mak' the best o' things,
Till in the end it's come to this :
　　Frae Phœbus reid upsprings,
Till she draps bleezin' yont the hill
　　I've aye a canty sang ;
There's nae a thing I buckle till
　　That can come to me wrang !
Like Scotia's sturdy thistle
Fowk may gang whine or whistle
　　Gin they keep clear o' me !
But roun' me come nae fykin'
Or welcome to their likin'
　　They're unco apt to pree !
But yet I dinna blame poor fowk
　　Wha hae but little lear',

And rain or shine maun scrape an' howk

To gather nocht but care,

Fae thinkin' whyles that Fortune's smiles

Are far frae pairtit fair ;

That mony a loon that wears a croon

A bonnet weel micht sair ;

And mony a chiel in poortith bides

That gin he had his due,

Would hae his girnal burstin' sides

His grey-beard foamin' fu' !

But wha can judge ?—he livesna here,

We are but finite things :

We see the burnie rinnin' clear

But kenna whaur it springs !

I'm nae a man to preach an' pray

Nor scoff at those that micht,

But I believe we'll see the day

Life's wrangs will be made richt.

Wi' watchfu' e'e on you and me

The Gaffir sits aboon :

The guid we dee,—the dunts we gie

Are in his book set doon.

Then let us work while bides the day

And strive e'er gloamin' comes,

In warp an' woof o' life to hae

The threids ootweigh the thrums;

And gin we a' would do our best,

Let that be great or sma',

And trust to Providence the rest,

Far wrang we couldna fa'!

O, Time unraivels mony hanks

To get but curses for her pranks,

But here am I will gie her thanks

As he'rtfelt as can be;

Let ithers fau't her gin they will

And ca' her ilka thing that's ill,

I'll toast her in my hinmost jill,

For she's been kind to me!"

"A GREAT NICHT THAT."

Sic pooer lay in the auld man's bow,
    He could put life in sticks an' stanes ;
    In truth, 'twas tauld that Geordie aince,
When comin' thro' the Quarry Howe,
    (Just as the clock in far Keith-ha'
    Boom'd out the eerie hoor o' twa,)
      Sat doon awhile to rest his banes ;
An' takin' " Tibbie " frae her nest,
    To wyle his weariness awa'
He gae the fiddle's breist a scrat,
An' ere ye could hae kissed the cat
    Aucht rubble rocks at his behest
Stood ready for a Highland reel.
Four were attired in broom and grass,
    An' four in crimson heather drest,

An' ilka carlin gat his lass
 An' took his kiss like gallant knicht,
When Geordie gar't his fiddle squeal,
 As prelude to the unco sicht.

There, in the silence o' the nicht,
 In hearin' o' the Bogie's croon,
 The clumsy craters, roun' an' roun',
Gaed whirlin' to the " Deil's Delicht."
They knapt their heels wi' siccan micht,
 The bawkie-birdies' heids cried stoun';
 The ools grew fleyt upon the trees ;
 The cushies croodl't to their young ;
For a' the glen like day was bricht
 An' flooded wi' an awesome soun'
 That, ghaist-like, wander't on the breeze
 Frae Quarry Hill to Corbie Tongue.

Twa hoors an' mair auld Geordie play'd,
 An' wow, he gart his fiddle sooch ;

Forbye the stanes, the trees, 'tis said,
  Were forced to crack their thooms and hooch.
An' dancin' there upon the green,
Till noo the fairies micht hae been,
  Were it no that the risin' sun
Loot fling his dairts an' fyled the fun.

Takin' his aim frae cauld Coreen,
  Red in the face wi' rage he slew
  The hale caboodle o' the crew—
Except, of coorse, his fiddlin' frien';
  He only looked at him an' leuch,
  An' said, "Weel, George, I've sneckt aneuch,
But dinna play sic pranks again."

"And what said you?" the laddies whiles
  Would speir whan Geordie tauld his tale
Some roarin' nicht aroun' the quiles,
  Wi' just a skyte o' nappy ale;

And George—oblivious to their smiles—

   Wad shout; " Wha yet has seen me quail ?

At sic a thocht my auld bluid biles ;

   To lairds or lords I dinna crooch.

" Their end's like mine—the nairrow trench,

   Their hungry heirs are gleg to tirr,

I took my snuff-mill frae my pooch

   An' yellacht—tho' I didna stir

Frae oot the bit a single inch :

   Guid mornin' to yer nichtcaip, sir ;

Wad ye no come an' tak' a pinch ? "

TO THE QUEEN *IN RE* THE VACANT LAUREATESHIP.

VICTORIA ! Tho' I hinna been
  For years at hame, 'tis true,
My native shire is Aberdeen,
  I'm proud to own it too ;
An' mair than a' yer still my Queen
  That I revere and lo'e,
So maybe I may be forgi'en
  If I dare sing to You !

Since first, adored by ilka class,
  Ye did the sceptre sway,
By Fortune it has come to pass
  That you've made Laureates tway :
O'er Wordsworth's narrow biel' the grass
  Has waved for mony a day,

And noo sweet Tennyson, alas,
　Has sung his hinmost lay !

Anither time ye hae the chance,
　O, blessin's on your name !
Some strugglin' minstrel to advance
　Upon the road to fame ;
And I for very joy would dance
　If he ye should proclaim,
To gie the office mair romance
　Cam' frae your Highland Hame !

Nae doot ye've lots o' Irish loons
　That fain would like the place,
And chiels in Welsh and English touns
　That weel the job could grace ;
But in the little Kingdom's boun's,
　I tell ye to your face,
For couthie, kindly sangs and tunes
　The Scotch can set the pace !

O, what can match auld Scotia's tongue
  For sweetness and for swing ?
Its Pathos frae the he'rt is wrung,
  Its Humor nane can ding !
And aye it comes frae auld or young
  Wi' sic a halesome ring
That whether written, preach'd or sung
  It stands o'er a' the bing !

As ye ken weel in days gane by
  The Doric held its ain
In lowly cot and castle high,
  Wi' courtier and wi' swain ;
But recently I'll no deny
  It has neglected lain,
And wad it no be weel to try
  To raise it up again ?

Within your veins there's Stuart blood,
  And it gave us Kings twa *

---

* James I. and James V.

That sang the Land o' Hill and Flood

In stirrin' strains and braw.

Tho' baith were nippit in the bud,

I wat they did nae sma',

But garr'd their numbers sweetly scud,

And bore the bell frae a' ! *

To let you hae your barest dues

My wonder you compel ;

And when ye gie's a bit o' news

Your style has sic a spell

Sometimes I think when I peruse

The stories that you tell,

That ye maun surely woo the Muse

And twang the Lyre yoursel' !

---

* A third, James VI. and I., we had, who wrote great skelps o'
rhyme, and while 'twas no sae unco bad, it wasna jist sublime !
But he's mair noted as the lad who did to Windsor climb, the
English to the Scots to add, in Willie Shakespeare's time ! The
Kings o' Albion lang had focht, the sister crown to gain, and truth
to tell 'twas aften thocht, had made the North their ain. But
Royal Jamie never socht wi' feuds to fash his brain, his Court he
just to Lunnon brocht, and started in to reign !

This much I ken : to Caledon
    You hae a tender he'rt,
And nane feel warmer to the Throne
    Than those frae Scotland's airt.
So may the happy bond stay on,
    Whatever else may pairt,
Till in the ages far ayon'
    Auld Time cowps owre its cairt !

Amang the poets that ye praise,
    Gin true what I hae heard,
Are some big dons that hae their claes
    Be-ribbon'd, cross'd and starr'd.
But since ye canna, tho' they fraise,
    The claims o' a' regard,
What would ye say to put the bays
    Upon a rustic bard ?

We've had nae lack o' Southrons noo
    Toon-bred and college-wise,

Aye gleg to laud wi' beck an' boo
　　Their patrons to the skies ;
So for a change ye micht alloo,
　　What Fair-play justifies,
A Scottish Country-Muse to pu'
　　For aince the laurell'd prize !

AN OLD TESTAMENT.

Whereas in life we are in death,
And know not when the hour may fall
When we must yield our mortal breath
And leave behind us here our all;
Whereas, while now I have the skill,
Resolved that I shall make my will!

Whereas it is the rule of late
To break a will for little cause,
That I may show my mental state
Is now as good as ere it was,
So none my saneness may asperse,
Resolved: I'll put my will in verse!

Imprimis, then, or simply First,
For that's the way the deeds begin,

All ye who hunger and who thirst
  To learn the facts enshrined herein,
Know straightway that my wits and health
Now constitute my chiefest wealth!

As in the plant we never see
  The fruits subsist without the stem,
These precious gifts must die with me,
  So none need wrangle over them;
Then thank the gods for what they gave,
And place my carcase in the grave!

The money that I have in bank,
  My Life Insurance funds, of course,
(I'll have to leave the totals blank!)
  And all my cash from every source
Now loaned or hoarded in my house,
I freely leave them to my spouse!

And if again she should not wed

    Before my bones to dust are turned,

I leave to her my second bed,

    My best one to be promptly burned,

Or else my ghost shall leave my tomb

And haunt her nightly in her room !

Should she precede me to her rest,

    I wish my wealth and all my wares

To pass, as justice might suggest,

    In equal sums and equal shares

Amongst our offspring that may live

When I my last farewell must give !

My books—I prize them more than gold !

    My letters, papers, all such things

I would not wish them to be sold,

    Such poor returns an auction brings ;

My child shall get them, I decree,

That most in taste resembles me !

My works in manuscript and print,

　In Scotch and English, verse and prose,

(If managed well might prove a mint,

　Tho' hardly likely, I suppose!)

I leave from first to final page

To readers of a future age!

My fame shall live, I here announce,

　Till Time be dead beyond a doubt;

Of course I hate to brag and bounce,

　But I might just as well speak out,

And pass my judgment on my lore,

For no one knows its value more!

And since in life I was denied

　A fitting seat to rest my bones,

My little fancies all decried,

　I want no monumental stones,

And in my grave let no one rake,

For Christ's—I mean for Jesus' sake!

My deepest curse upon the ——

Who pose as patrons of the Arts,

And yet permit rare —— ——

To hawk around in cadgers' carts ;

Who rave o'er poets long since dead,

And let the live ones beg for bread !

With this advice impress your mind,

O man or woman money-rich,

If chance should lead you forth to find

A genius drudging in the ditch,

Disburse a portion of your pelf

And give him help to help himself !

A cent thus spent would far outweigh

A million doled to spread the fame

Of some Immortal wrapped in clay,

I care not how you spell his name :

Who can assist old Homer now

Or add a laurel to his brow ?

But when he jogg'd from door to door
 In Grecian Gaberlunzie style,
And was repulsed like many more
 As if he were a vagrant vile,
Then was the time to lend him aid—
And so, I guess, enough's been said !

These rugged lines should any read,
 And think my drift is hardly plain,
I say they may come better speed
 If they peruse the piece again ;
I have not time to prune and graft
Like experts of the legal craft !

I name as my executrix ——
 (Here melted wax had spoiled a line)—
At fifty *(blot)* her bonds I fix,
 Bear witness as my name I sign
(Another blot) in order due,
On August third of 'Ninety-two !

AN ADDRESS TO THE AUTHOR OF "PRESS CHIPS."*

CHIPPER chappie, take my thanks,
 I shall sing a song to thee
For thy witty quips and cranks
 Indiscriminatory!

Justly worthy of applause,
 In a million readers' eyes,
Chieftain of the Chip-pewas,
 Catachresticallywise!

Sparkling Anonymity,
 Punch-inello of the Press,
Rarely in thy style we see
 Disproportionableness!

---

* A daily series of unsigned versicles in various moods and measures which appeared in the Philadelphia " Press " during the summer of 1889.

Rains descend or Phœbus shine,
  Boreas blow or Zephyr sigh,
Every chip is stamped with thine
  Individuality !

For the fellows such as I,
  Who admire thy comic chaff,
Wont you kindly publish thy
  Photochromolithograph ?

Merrily as marriage bells
  Ring thy notes from A to Zº, *
Sweet and strong as Philomel's,
  Inimitability !

Than myself thy daily log
  With more gusto never cons,
Sesquipedal pedagogue—
  Parallelopipedons !

---

* American pronunciation—"Zee."

Than thy title, happier thought
  Reader never ran across,
Since the days when Carey wrote
  " Chrononhotonthologos."

Since the times of more renown,
  When without a fleck or flaw
Musing Milton scribbled down
  " Areopagitica."

Since the era, greater still,
  When our Shakespeare made a fuss
With " Honorificabil—
  Itudinitatibus ! "

And thy courage !—one might seek
  Just as soon to knock away
Popocatepetl's peak's
  Perpendicularity !

Nye, the Prince of Jesters called,
  Nigh thee placed, experts confess,
Tumbles headlong into *bald*
  Insignificativeness.

Jack-a-dandy of the types,
  View'd beside thee, ev'n Pan,
Seems a—yes, for all his pipes—
  Valetudinarian !

Some there are (who envies such !)
  Deem you funny in excess,
Think your jingles show too much
  Tintinnabulariness !

Prosy bores, with noodles null,
  Who can but expect from these
Incommensurably dull
  Comprehensibilities ?

Check your rhyme and rhythm too ?

    Curb your jaunty jollity ?—

When the rush-light can outdo

    Pyroelectricity !

Would your critics find a cure

    For their dreary pessimism ?

Let them try a shock of your

    Antihypochondraism !

Verse is not a penal fault,

    (Hear me shrews and cynics all !)

Nor a pinch of Attic salt

    Anticonstitutional,

Dolichocephalic chap,

    Long may you be spared to chip,

Free from Talent's worst mishap—

    Maladministratorship !

To the bards a beacon light

In the stereotyped abyss,

Coruscating like a bright

Carbovegetabilis !

Long be spared thy verses all,

Hypercatalectic woe,

Unencyclopaedical

Improvisatorio ! *

---

* For this poem can be claimed at least *originality of measure*, ·
and the same may be said for the poems beginning pp. 3 and 27,
not a trifling feat at this late date in the development of rhyme
and rhythm.

A PRAYER.

WHEN comes the time—as come it may—
(Tho' lang the Lord prevent it !)
Good folks to ae puir meal a day,
   Nae maitter whaur, are stintit ;—
Wi' meat an' drink as scant an' scarce
   As Truth is in Tradition,
Grand Sutler o' the Universe
   This shall be my petition :—

Let Brother Bull get Roasts and Fries,
   Wi' Ale and Porter handy ;
Gie France her Soups and Puddock Pies,
   And bottles fu' o' Brandy ;
Gie Sauer-kraut to the Dutch Grandees,
   And Rhine wine till they stagger ;

Gie Prussians Sausages and Cheese

Wi' Flasks o' foamin' Lager ;

Gie Jonathan his Buckwheat Cake,

His Pumpkin an' Tomatoes,

His Soda drinks that never slake ;

Gie Paddy his potatoes ;

Gie Italy her Oils an' Spice

And fragrant Maccaroni ;

Gie poppies, Birdies' Nests and Rice

To pig-tailed Jap or Johnny ;

Gie Swedish Turnips to the Swedes,

To Poles gie Roley-Poleys ;—

To ilka Nation gie its needs,

Forgetting fau'ts an' follies,—

Deal oot an' dinna hain ;

As lang's ye leave your loyal SCOTS

In porridge plates and pewter pots

The Flesh and Blood o' juicy OATS

To stap their kytes an' weet their throats

They never shall complain !

TO WED OR NOT TO WED?—THAT IS
THE QUESTION!

I FIND, on reading of the undertaking,

 That Men of Genius since the world began

Have found in Marriage less of joy than aching,

 As we can gather if their lives we scan.

These illustrations, from a random raking

 Amongst the records of the writing clan,

I simply quote as I delight to sprinkle

Great names on paper and to hear them tinkle!

Old Mrs. Dante, who could likely hem a

 Chemise or handkerchief exceeding well,

Was less a jewel than she was a Gem-ma:

 If we can swallow what traditions tell

Her tongue was frightful, can we then condemn a
    Revengeful Poet if he wrote on " Hell,"
And formed his periods in a style more graphic
Than he could muster for his theme seraphic ?

The Bard of Avon was entrapped in youth
    By quite an elderly and portly lady,
And Shakespeare's habits, to declare the truth,
    And put it mildly, were a bit unsteady ;
His life in London was reverse of smooth,
    His home affections were a trifle shady,
And judging from his Sonnets I should say
He did not dote upon Ann Hathaway !

The pious Milton was a fraud we gather,
    In spite of all his hymning and his creeds ;
His first wife left him in a hurry rather
    Than shape her conduct to his peevish needs ;
With Number Two he proved a careless father
    And left his daughters to grow up like weeds,

Small wonder then, to aggravate his woes,

He found in Wedlock more of Thorn than Rose !

Montaigne was happy when he left his spouse,

   He looked on marriage as domestic pain,

It is recorded, as his vow of vows,

   With Wisdom's self he would not wed again ;

John Dryden's wife brought discord to his house,

   She was so cross and cranky in the grain ;

And Moliere—as well as writer Rousseau—

Deplored the day he saw a bridal trousseau !

Spectator Joe, from whom the tyro strives

   The heights and depths of English speech to learn,

Put in the wretchedest of wedded lives,

   His ancient Countess gave him much concern,

And proved an equal to the testy wives

   Of tatler Steele and sentimental Sterne,

While Mrs. Coleridge tied with Churchill's mate

In running races for the Vixen Plate !

The great Lord Byron made a mess of marriage,
   His honeymoon he called a " treacle-moon ; "
'Twas Bulwer's pride his partner to disparage,
   And Dickens deem'd a single life a boon ;
But bliss came also in Minerva's carriage,
   Some clever couples have been known to spoon,
All writers were not like Carlyle the crusty,
Who snubb'd his dearie till her love grew rusty !

Sir Walter Raleigh led a sweet existence,
   Admired and solaced by his youthful wife ;
Sir Francis Bacon, tho' he kept his distance
   From Lady Bacon, kept away from strife ;
The Scotch Sir Walter, with a rare persistence,
   Remained a lover till the end of life,
And Burns the poet, from his life we glean,
Was ever singing of his bonnie Jean !

Wordsworth and Southey, and melodious Moore,
   (And Shelley, too, upon the second trial),

In spite of all their lyrics and their lore,

    Were happy husbands there is no denial;

The Halls and Howitts did not deem a bore

    The draughts they quaff'd from Matrimony's phial,

And who could slander the contentment crowning

The married life of Bob and Mrs. Browning?

Sweet Henry Wadsworth and the Concord Sage,

    The honey'd Hawthorne of "The Scarlet Letter,"

And Russell Lowell, of a later age,

    Were all believers in the silken fetter;

'Twould take the compass of an ample page

    To name the authors made by wedlock better;

But then, again, what lives have there been prettier

That those of Whitman and his compeer Whittier?*

---

* Both bachelors.

INVOKING THE MUSE.

In my restricted, interrupted leisure,
To woo the Muses is my chiefest pleasure,
But then, with duties that I need not mention,
My wife and babies must have some attention !

I'M stuck, by thunder !—I may now confess it,

My luck has brought me to a pretty pickle !

An evening gone without a verse to bless it ;

Why, fickle fortune, should you prove so fickle ?

I take my matter and I try to dress it,

I tug and tussle till the sweat-drops trickle—

My steed poetic in a fit has flunk'd,

And for a stanza I'm completely skunk'd !

You see—and possibly I should have noted

The facts I give you ere to this I came—

I'm not a member of the broad-cloth-coated

"Association of the SONS OF FAME ;"

In time amongst them I may get promoted,

   But for the present I can make no claim,

I drudge at writing for an occupation,

And rhyming's nothing but my recreation !

    .   .   .   .

And now I'm stuck !—but I shall tell the reason,

   Quite unconcerned about the consequences,

It's now the springtime and the cleaning season,

   And I've been working to cut down expenses ;

I guess 'twas something like poetic treason,

   And what I'd scouted in my sober senses,

But, press'd and pester'd, for the time I wilted

Renounced the Muses—and I find I'm jilted !

I lifted carpets and I shifted stoves,

   I netted pictures and I scrubbed and dusted,

Mosquitoes routed by the dozen droves,

   Put screens in windows and the doors adjusted ;

I sprinkled coffee and I scatter'd cloves,

   And disinfected, till at last disgusted

I vowed I should not be in any hurry
To waste my time in such another flurry!

Then came the tussle in our little garden :
   The neighbours hinting that it should be sodded,
I did my utmost in attempts to harden
   My flabby muscles as I nightly plodded
At digging, delving, and at hauling sward in ;
   And thus it pays me or I may be clodded,
For all the velvet that I've cut and carted
It's barer now than when before I started !

A Rhymester's something like an acrobatic
   Or juggling artist—he must practise ever ;
If in performance he becomes erratic
   He'll lose his balance, or he's extra clever :
And so I'm sticking in my little attic,
   Unblest with verse because I had to sever
My close connection with poetic style,
And leave Parnassus for a little while !

But I'll do better in the time to come,

    And naught shall tempt me from my love to stray ;

Then why, O Muses, will ye still be glum?

    Without your favours I may quit my lay ;

But smile upon me and we'll make things hum,

    I'm all impatient to resume the play :

Gee up, O Pegasus, or I, perforce,

Will have to hustle for another horse !

A DIG AND A DIGRESSION.

O FEW—which is the same as "far between"—
　Are men with pluck enough to take a stand
And do a thing before they yet have seen
　If other folks have lent a helping hand;
They use a precedent by way of screen,
　In case a critic should by chance demand
The why and wherefore of a strange transaction,
As if a precedent could screen an action!

It's not amiss to know what others do:
　I read the poets who have gone before me;
Some please my fancy, it is very true,
　But many others (I confess it) bore me;
The simpler singers I can struggle thro',
　The mystic writers with their riddles floor me;

A rhyme I fancy may become my model,

But it would never enter in my noddle

To ask my Muses if I should have leave

(Presuming always that I had ability)

An untried rhythm in my verse to weave,

For that too much would savour of servility :

To link my octaves is a thing, I grieve,

I've done it just to show with what facility

I can accomplish such a feat, because

It's now the fashion to bestow applause

On poetasters of the present crop,

Who must imagine it betokens skill

Across the channels of the page to hop,

The subdivision of the verse to kill,

And think it's brilliant to insert a stop

Right in the stanza's centre with their quill !

To me such writers by their writings teach

The form they tackle is beyond their reach,

And they might just as well descend to prose

As hack their measures in a way so vile.

The proper method, as a schoolboy knows,

   In contradiction to the current style,

Is for the poet at the verse's close

   To isolate each stanza like an isle,

And let the reader at the pauses snatch

An opportunity his breath to catch !

No further this digression to prolong,

   Which we have follow'd for a verse or two,

As I have stated, there is nothing wrong

   In being posted on what others do ;

A man will rarely run against a prong

   If past experience he keeps in view ;

But were we all to be of such a sort

What little progress could the world report !

Hotch-Potch (in English and Scotch).

Being versicles on various Topics, including Impromptus, Epigrams, Comments, Criticisms, Inscriptions, etc.

M. AURELIUS ANTONINUS,
   In discussing " Early Rising,"
To Lie Still he must design us,
   Recommending Moralizing.
While a fellow's cogitating
   He's averse to stir a stump,
And instead of thus debating
   'Tis the better way to—JUMP !

——*0*——

O ye who Clothing simply scan,
Be careful how you judge a man :
Beneath most uninviting ground
The richest ores are often found !

——*0*——

Those writers show the greatest sense
        That can condense.
Their gifts are of the highest sort,
        That " cut it short."

Of pithy rules for scribbling fools,
    In my belief,
    This is the chief :
    BE BRIEF !

——o——

While as a rule we should not show
  A spark of animosity,
Against whatever has the glow
  Or gleam of generosity ;
It positively is a crime
For any man to waste our time
With dreary screeds of prose or rhyme,
  Enveloped in verbosity !

——o——

Clearness, Correctness and Condensation,
Is the three-hued happy combination
That would much improve the bad condition
Of many a heavy Composition !

——o——

When one considers now-a-days
  With what great assiduity
Our poets decorate their lays
  With gems of ambiguity,
They should receive the highest praise
  Who have the ingenuity
To run against the current craze,
  And write with perspicuity !

——o——

From careful observation
And knowledge of tuition,
I make this proclamation :
(Forgive the ebullition !)
The Laws and Rules of Grammar
Not worth a tinker's dam are,*
Compared to *Imitation*
For learning Composition !

ON PERUSING FOR THE FIRST TIME THE POEMS OF ALEXANDER WILSON.

EPISTLE TO J. D.

There's mony a warm inspirin' screed
Sprung frae a whiskey potion,
But, Sandy, lad, nae jill ye need
To set your Muse in motion !
Some Bards could never catch your leed
When rhymin' tak's your notion,
Tho' they held bumpers to their heid
As bigs the German Ocean
In bulk this day !

THE PACK.

Weel spoken, Wilson, witty chiel !—
Weel spoken, Pedlar's pack !

---

* Gentle reader : I'm not swearing ! a " dam " is worth a little more than a bawbee.

19

A century has turned its wheel
  Sin' ye begood your crack !
An' hunners yet thro' space may reel,
  Yea, Time gang a' to wrack,
Ere cauld Oblivion set its seal
  On sic a canty trac'
               For aince and aye !

EPISTLE TO A BROTHER PEDLAR.

LANG, lang, O Pedlars hae ye pass'd
  Into your hinmost hame,
And cares for aye ahint ye cast
  On dainties to your wame ;
So I'll nae wish your backs boo'd doun
  Wi' snag to mortals giv'n,
But rowth o' a' that gangs the roun'
  As lang's ye bide in Heav'n,
             I humbly pray !

CALLAMPHITRE'S ELEGY.

AYE, sleeps he soun' as ony carl,
  O'er-maister'd by a drappie ;
But dootna in anither warl'
  He's wide awauk an' happy ;
And never can he be forgot,
  Nor negligence enthral him,
While here there bides a kilted Scot
  That dances Ghillie-Callum,
           By Nicht or Day !

EPISTLE TO MR. W. M.

WAS Fortune kind or crookit mou'd
When sic a wye she used ye?—
Nae doot gin there we would hae voo'd
She sairly had abused ye ;
But noo we're less inclined to ban
For had the Tup done better,
And gin the gowd had graced your han'
We michtna had sic Letter
To read this day !

EPISTLE TO A. C.

SANDY, Sandy ! You're a dandy,
And I gang nae far amiss,
When I swear that rhymin' Andie
Never wrote the peer o' this !

EPISTLE TO J. D.

A BONNY picture o' the toun,
As fresh as saut sea breezes ;
My fegs ye are a clever loon
And never fail to please us !
Awa'—at hame
It's a' the same
When ye set to your story ;
In ilka line
Sae fine ye shine,
We canna but encore ye !

EPISTLE TO J. K.

Why, why, O Wilson, did ye dee,
And live sae lang ahead o' me?
Your tastes and mine so grandly gree
　　　I'd nae rebel
To shouther wi' a chiel like thee
　　　The Pack mysel'!

VIRGIL'S CAUTION TO THE READER.

When o'er a rhyme ae blink ye tak'
　　Ye only get a taste o't,
And twenty times ye maun gang back
　　Or ye possess the best o't!

THE REEL O' STUMPIE.

Willie Creech, aince Provost Creech, in Edinbroch,
　　the city o't,
To pass his time made up this rhyme,—the muckle
　　mair's the pity o't;
For gin the gowk had thocht to gang and gi'en to Burns,
　　a teetie o't
We micht hae had a better sang to "Wap an' Rowe the
　　Feetie o't!"

A PREFACE TO "HOLY WILLIE'S PRAYER."

The printer chiel's been unco fasheous,
And fu' o' auld-wife wishy-washes
To mak' a mess o' docket dashes
    This pious pleadin';
Sic wyes o' work are far frae cautious
    And sair misleadin',
So I hae stappit up the gashes
    To mak' richt readin'!

SCOTLAND'S TRINITY—BURNS, FERGUSSON, RAMSAY.

Nae Southron loon but maun alloo
The Muses hae been partial to
    The Land o' Cakes an' Thistles;
And Robert Burns to thee belangs
The Chieftainship for Scottish Sangs,
    For Poems and Epistles!
I aince was browden't on your book,
    And yet I wyte I am sae!
But, lad, I canna weel o'erlook
    The debt ye owe to Ramsay.
      Thy rhymes saft at times aft
        Frae Fergusson's are swallen,
      But daringly and glaringly
      Ye've stown frae " gentle " Allan!

TIME'S VERDICT.

BONNIER burnies may I see,
Bonnier howes may greet my e'e,
Dearer nane can ever be
    Than Bogie and Strath-Bogie !

" THE TWA DOGS."

A WEEL-TAULD easy-goin' tale,
A " jinglin " Geordie I'se be bail !
And, Robert, wise thou wert indeed
To start your bookie wi' this screed.
It shows sic thochtfu', musin' airt,
It maun hae ta'en the puir fowks he'rt !
" Here " ye would force them to confess,
" Here we hae fand in hamely dress
A Poet worthy to be placed
Amang the sweetest and the best
That ever warbled here below !—
A Makkar, three times sworn the foe
O' a' that's wrang in man to man ;
A hame-owre singer, ane that can
Wile us a while frae cark and care ;
Whose verse like waughts o' caller air
Sweeps oot the cob-webs in oor brains,
And like the kindly summer rains
That freshen up the dorby lan'
Puts vigor in oor head an' han' !" etc., etc.

A CONTRIBUTION TO THE BOOKS' CONTROVERSY.

THE best book yet is the—Pocket-Book ;
The Book of Books is the Pocket-Book ;
The Pocket-Book when a well-filled Book
    Is a Book that few despise !

"AS A RULE."

The best Impromptus still are those
Conceived and born in cloister'd close,
    When Sol drops under Terra's keel
        And swings on Space his dead-light ;
    Those sharpen'd on the *pen*-sive steel
        And polish'd up with *head*-light !

" TULLOCHGORUM."

O, SKINNER, sweetly hast thou sung :
Thy verse tho' auld is ever young ;
'Twill live as lang's our Mither-Tongue,
    Or Scot wears Bonnet o'er him ;
" First of Lyrics " Burns confest—
First of Lyrics—first of Lyrics—
First of Lyrics Burns confest—
    Land-melody or jorum ;
First of Lyrics, Burns confest,
By "first" of course he meant THE BEST,
And nane will better stan' the test
    Than thy rare " Tullochgorum ! "

TO THOSE WHO LIKE TO STRUT ABOUT—AND SPEAK—AND SPOUT.

THE gift of gab's a doubtful gift
With which to turn a man adrift,
For he who likes to wag his jaw
Is very apt to thrash old straw,
And tempt his friends to criticize :
Say little and you'll pass for wise !

——o——

There's " luck in leisure " some folk say,
 I hold the *saw* of small accompt,
Believing 'tis the better way
 In all transactions to be prompt !

——o——

" Assume it if you have it not "
 Applies to any sort of stuff ;
The Real's not by Sham begot,
 But Credit is the Child of Bluff !

——o——

Make up your mind, if mind you've got,
 And when you see your duty clear,
Tho' zeal get cold that once was hot,
 ADHERE and PERSEVERE !

DON'T BE FINICAL!

I GRANT you that it's very nice
In most of things to be precise ;
   I also will admit 'tis meet
   To try to have a thing complete ;
But do your best and acquiesce
Or daily you'll accomplish less,
   And idly will your time be spent
   If you give way to discontent !

KEEP UP TO THE TIMES.

IN this mad hustling bustling age
The man who would with Fortune wage
   The most successful war,
In little and in big affairs
Must waste no wind in climbing stairs
   Where Elevators are !

We cannot deem a spendthrift wise
   Howe'er his acts we view ;
A stingy man we all despise
   'Tis also very true.
But in the end he'll win, say I,
   Who keeps back in reserve,
The largest and the best supply
   Of nickels and of nerve !

'Tis better to admit the fact—
　　We cannot all be great ;
　It is the forte of some to act
　　Of others to create.
And some again are very good
　　At finding faults and flaws,
But woe betide the ones who should
　　Yet will not give applause !

———o———

Bannocks o' bear-meal, bannocks o' barley,
Here's to the Highlandman's bannocks o' barley ;
Plump is the lassie and stout is the carlie
Fed on the bannocks o' bear-meal an' barley !

AN OBSERVATION.

PERSISTENT dropping will outwear a stone :
　　Let critics sneer and let the cynics snicker,
It may be for the sake of peace alone,
　　But all things tumble to the constant kicker ;
The louder also that you make your moan
　　Relief will hurry to your side the quicker ;
A nurse may dally with a sleepy dunce,
A squalling baby must be soothed at once !

NOTHING SUCCEEDS LIKE SUCCESS.

O, WHAT fantastic idiotic pranks
 A man may play if he can play to win !
The more grotesque he gets the better thanks,
 Even doubtful tricks are varnished with a grin ;
But woe betide the innovating cranks
 That make a failure as their tops they spin ;
With that derision Mrs. Grundy views
The poor unfortunates that play to lose !

THE GOSPEL OF DRESS.

HE was a convert to the worldly creed
 That Clothes an applicant can mar or make ;
That Beggars always can come better speed
 In almost anything they undertake,
If they will deck them in a fitting weed :
 Dame Fortune's gifts are scatter'd in the wake
Of booby dandies, while a man of brain
In poor apparel will appeal in vain !

AN INTERLUDE.

Now westward Phoebus with his fiery car
 Has made his exit in a blaze of red ;
Beneath the shadows of the spires afar
 The river flashes like a silver thread ;
The moon attended by a single star
 Is softly shining from the blue o'erhead ;
But while I'm partial to the picturesque,
I guess I'll hie me to my writing desk !

A NOTE TO A FAMOUS POEM.

WHETHER as Linguist or as Lyrist view'd,
  Lord Byron's worthy of all commendation ;
For "chew'd," 'tis true, he sometimes said "eschew'd,"
  A curious error in his education ;
But at the Spanish he was surely crude
  When he implied that the pronunciation
Of "Juan" (as in "Don Juan") should be like "Jew-
    one,"
  When "Whan" or "Wan" is, for a fact, the true one!

'TWAS EVER THUS.

LIKE many more, he had begun to learn
  The world's mistrustful of a thing that's new ;
Long years of waiting and repulses stern
  The best Inventions have to struggle thro'
Before a dollar they can hope to earn,
  And many failures by the way ensue :
With books, with creeds, with everything, in fact,
A new departure shows a want of tact !

Our modern samples of successes prove
  (Look round about you and you'll see it's so)
The men who labour in a well-worn groove
  Seem everywhere to get a better show
Than clever fellows who are prone to move
  In contradiction to the general flow ;
Great praise is shower'd upon Originality,
  For cash—Conformity's the better quality !

SMALL DETAILS.

Iт may look trivial to be too precise,
    And needless trifling we should seek to stifle,
But laconism is a greater vice,
    And abstract writers should receive a rifle ;
It's little things that give the spark and spice,
    That make perfection—which is not a trifle ;
While brevity may be the soul of wit,
Long-winded fellows make the greatest hit !

WHITHER?

In vain we cry for further licht,
    In vain we seek the veil withdrawn ;
But as the day leads on to nicht,
    And nicht again gives place to dawn,
So, dootless, will the end come richt,
And darkness yield to mornin' bricht !

SECURITY.

Aн ! who need fear the Tempest's shock
Whose house is grounded on a rock ?
What ghost dare seek to follow him
Who keeps his lamp in perfect trim ?
And—who may bless or who may ban—
What harm can hurt an HONEST MAN ?

One unpretentious kindly deed
Is worth a life of empty creed !

AU REVOIR!

WHY finer spin my simple rhyme
And spoil your temper and your time?
Frae what I've done it's only fair
To grant I'm fit for something mair,
As (luck be praised!) when said is a'
I'm twenty-aucht, nae auchty-twa;
And what you've seen and what you see
Is but the bloom upon the tree
That shows whaur fruit may yet be twined
Gin Chance and Fate prove halflins kind!

APPENDICES.

A.

*" A Dream o' Hame" (Geographical), was originally dedicated
to G. W. Anderson, of the Seaforth Highlanders, on receipt of his
" Lays of Strathbogie and the Story of the Strath ;" and concluded
with the following lines :—*

> Such are the scenes portray'd by you,
> O Minstrel sweet and Artist true !
> Altho' your face I've never seen
> I feel that I can ca' ye frien'.
> For this braw book ye've sent to me
> I waft my thanks across the sea.
> "THE STORY O' THE STRATH " shall stand
> While Noth o'ertaps the Gordon land,
> And Bogie as it wanders on
> Shall sing the praise of ANDERSON !

*The following selected extracts refer to only a few of the Poems
in this volume, the greater portion of the book being printed for the
first time :—*

B.

" DEAR SIR,—I thank you for your communication, particularly
the interesting paraphrase of Psalm I. I am happy to find the
Scottish dialect has crossed the water. As to the small matter of
my nationality the facts are clear. I was born in Liverpool. My
father and mother and all my forbears were Scotch exclusively.
Your faithful and obdt. servt.,

"W. E. GLADSTONE."

C.

"Your rich geographical ditty. If I had influence with the
educators of the people in that quarter, I should certainly advise
that the verses should be recited and sung in every school between
the Dee and the Deveron. . . . A true poet, as the lines to
Sherman prove. The 'Domestic Duet' is a good piece of broad
humour, and thrown off with the fresh dramatic touch from real
life, for which Scottish song is so famous.

"(PROFESSOR) JOHN STUART BLACKIE."

" My Dear Friend,—I have read with pleasure thy ' Dream
o' Hame '—the dream which thousands of Scotch born Americans
I doubt not are dreaming. I honour them for their undying love
of their broomy knowes and heathery hills. With many thanks
for thy poem, I am, thy aged friend,

"JOHN G. WHITTIER."

" My Dear Sir,—I thank you sincerely for your kindness in
sending me a copy of your "Dream o' Hame," which I have not
had the chance of reading till this evening. It has given me great
pleasure, and of that refined pleasure, too, which is not unakin to
pain. There is pervading it a wail of home-sickness and of intense
yearning for the vanished years and vanished places which corres-
ponds to the minor key that is dominant in genuine Scotch music.
Again thanking you for the real pleasure you have given me, I beg
to remain, dear sir, yours respectfully,

"HORACE HOWARD FURNESS."

" Your braw hame-poem is a wholesome lilt as well as musical,
and I thank you soundly for the copy you have personally marked
for me. But a brief while ago I browsed the Burns-land over—
learning there to even love the 'poemer' better than before—and
his country and his people—though inordinately fond of all of them
since old enough to read. Again my heartiest thanks for your ain
hinnied sang, and believe me very cordially your friend,

"JAMES WHITCOMB RILEY."

" Your truly spirited panoramic poem. . . . A Highland
heart, or sentiment if you will, breathes all through your production,
and that you include so many place-names gives a rare value to the
piece.

"DUNCAN MACGREGOR CRERAR."

" I have read your 'Dream o' Hame' more than once with
interest and pleasure. Your mastery of the dear old Doric is
undeniable, and your enumeration of the many finely sounding
burns, rivers, hills and clachans is grateful to me. . . . A
noble old bard, Isaiah, forty centuries before our day, understood
as no modern rhymester does the peculiar value of sonorous and
magnificent names.

"THOMAS C. LATTO."

" I have read it several times and certainly each time with more
pleasure. It is very graphic—all the pictures clearly defined, and
not an inharmonious line in the whole poem.

"ALEX. ANDERSON (Surfaceman)."

" Spirited !—GENERAL JAMES GRANT-WILSON."

" Graceful.—LORD ABERDEEN."

" Characteristic.—OLIVER WENDELL HOLMES."

" DEAR MR. C.,—You have done me a rare kindness in sending me the 'Dream o' Hame.' Nearly every mountain and place named I have visited or passed so near that I felt very much at hame with the portrayal from first to last. Only a born poet could have interpreted the 'cycloramic view' with so many gems. Is it any wonder I find the eloquent commentary as succulent as graphic ? " W. P. M."

" Read with interest and pleasure.—JOHN S. KENNEDY."

" Charming 'Dream o' Hame !' You have cleverly put together the panorama of a beautiful Scotch landscape, where every scene is associated with romance or history.
" REV. E. C. BOLLES (D.D.)."

" The Scotch lines inscribed to me are far too flattering, but I shall swallow them, and try to outflank the deil for some years yet.
" GENERAL SHERMAN (to CARNEGIE)."

" DEAR JAMIE,—It is a paraphrase to be proud of. Auld Rouse would have accepted it with as fair a joy as could be expected from one who had surpassed him in his own special line. . . . I love the homely Doric Scotch which smacks so of the soil and the spirit. . . . Brood over a few of the choicest of the old Psalms, and when they sing to you in the mother tongue as this has sung, try again. Indeed yours,
" ROBERT COLLYER (D.D.)."

" MY DEAR FRIEND,—Much obliged to you for the copy of your excellent poem on Walt Whitman. It shows that you have 'a spark of Nature's fire.' . . . I hope to see you in Phila. on the 21st. Thanking you again and again, I remain, as ever, your friend,
" (COLONEL) R. G. INGERSOLL."

" Your leading good quality is the natural, spontaneous, easy-going flow of words that happily round themselves into lyrical form. Spontaneity is the perfection of all art and the hardest to attain. In this you are not excelled by any Scottish poet of our time. . . . Your Scotch is the purest of any I know in America.

. . . The paraphrase of the First Psalm is the best thing of its kind I ever read. . . . Very few can appreciate it fully. They are prone to see humour in it. To me it seems sanctified by memories of the Covenant, and is such as Knox might have read in St. Giles.

"JAMES KENNEDY, Author of
"'Scottish American Poems,' 'The Deeside Lass,' etc."

"It is certainly quite a remarkable production. Mr. Law's command of language is extraordinary. . . . I have read his poem 'A Nicht wi' Burns' a good many times and have enjoyed it very much. . . . I shall take great pleasure in making his acquaintance.

"(DR.) JAS. MAC ALISTER
"(President of Drexel Institute)."

"A true poet. . . . Will not discredit Scotland.
"ANDREW CARNEGIE."

www.ingramcontent.com/pod-product-compliance
Lightning Source LLC
Chambersburg PA
CBHW060525030726
47498CB00004B/1078